*Look what people are saying about
this talented author....*

"Enthralling...a great plot, a wonderful hero
and heroine, and sense of history make
a totally outstanding book."
—*RT Book Reviews* on *The Captive*

"Expect fireworks."
—*Night Owl Reviews* on *Manhunting*

"Joanne Rock never fails to impress!"
—*Writers Unlimited* on
She Thinks Her Ex Is Sexy...

"Joanne Rock has a home run of a hit with
four sexy, hotter-than-hot players."
—Suzanne Coleburn,
The Belles & Beaux of Romance,
on *Sliding into Home*

"Four fabulous tales! The sex is scorching and
the four couples are engaging and entertaining."
—*Romance Reviews Today* on *Sliding into Home*

"Scrumptious."
—*Cataromance* on *Sliding into Home*

Dear Reader,

Baseball season is more than the great American pastime around my house. With three sons and a husband who hails from a family of seven sports-crazy brothers (and one sister who learned at an early age how to hold her own), I spend a lot of time at the ballpark in the summer. Opening day of baseball is a holiday that warrants calling in sick, and a good game on the West Coast is worth staying up until 1:30 in the morning to watch.

But while I'm rooting for the home team, chances are far more likely that I'm dreaming up stories for those nine guys who takes the field. Being a Blaze writer, I can have their lives turned around by romance in a heartbeat!

Aces' manager Heath Donovan doesn't need much help from me to find his life in a tailspin, however. And he flat-out refuses to be a trophy boyfriend for the sexy siren next door after she mistakes him for the Aces' playboy third baseman. Good thing book reviewer Amber Nichols takes her manhunting very seriously once she sets her mind to it. She's not about to let her hot prospect get away....

I hope you enjoy *Double Play*. Don't forget to look for sneak peeks from my upcoming releases at www.joannerock.com!

Happy reading,

Joanne Rock

Joanne Rock

DOUBLE PLAY

TORONTO • NEW YORK • LONDON
AMSTERDAM • PARIS • SYDNEY • HAMBURG
STOCKHOLM • ATHENS • TOKYO • MILAN • MADRID
PRAGUE • WARSAW • BUDAPEST • AUCKLAND

Recycling programs
for this product may
not exist in your area.

ISBN-13: 978-0-373-79564-2

DOUBLE PLAY

www.eHarlequin.com

Printed in U.S.A.

ABOUT THE AUTHOR

Three-time RITA® Award nominee and Golden Heart winner Joanne Rock is the author of more than forty books for Harlequin. A fan of both medieval historicals and sexy contemporaries, she is particularly thrilled to pen her first Harlequin Blaze Historical novel, set in a medieval period. When she's not writing or spending too much time on Facebook, Joanne teaches English at the local university to share her love of the written word in all its forms. For more information, visit Joanne at www.joannerock.com.

Books by Joanne Rock

For Dean, who doesn't suffer baseball
mistakes lightly—even in fiction. Thank you
for helping me with my logistics!

Prologue

*IF EVER THERE WAS an ideal man for a fling, it would be
the hot baseball player next door.*

Amber Nichols recalled her best friend's words, blaring in her ear like an iPod on full blast, as the male in
question emerged from the surface of Nantucket Sound
like a modern-day Poseidon. Amber watched him from
the deck of Rochelle's home on Great Point, overlooking
the water. Her former college roommate had generously
offered her the beach house more than once during their
decade-long friendship, an offer Amber had only accepted now that her life was imploding.

In the course of two months, she'd weathered a
wretched breakup and major cutbacks at the newspaper
where she worked as a book reviewer. While the breakup
had torn at her heart, the cutbacks left her overworked
and fearing for her job, leading to stress, exhaustion and
shaken confidence all the way around.

Here, she could regroup and relax. Open a new

chapter in her life that didn't involve playing it safe and overthinking every decision.

Of course, Rochelle had given Amber plenty of dating advice along with the keys to the place, convinced a wild affair would cure what ailed her. She had never understood Amber's penchant for practical, methodical men who approached life with the same sense of caution that Amber did. But then, Rochelle had never met Amber's perpetually heartbroken mom who had taught Amber the wisdom of holding something of yourself back. Amber simply made dating choices that reflected that.

Dating choices that still seemed to backfire just as surely as her mother's had, although for entirely different reasons. Obviously, something wasn't working with her approach. But Amber wasn't sure she was ready to take Rochelle's advice during her week of transformation and rest.

Rochelle had been particularly effusive in her description of the studly third baseman for the Boston Aces staying next door. Apparently the club's manager owned the house and frequently let various team members stay there as a perk.

The sleekly muscled male was living up to Rochelle's hype. The setting sun caught the rivulets streaming along his skin, making his bronzed body glisten. No slow-motion movie sequence had ever been more flattering to the masculine physique. His square, powerful shoulders were even more mouthwatering as he lifted his arms to wipe his hair from his face. Even from the front of him, she could see the muscles that would form the V of his back.

Her gaze followed that enticing stretch of sinew as she straightened, moving closer to the wooden railing of the raised deck as if drawn by a magnet. Taut abs flexed as he walked, each slab clearly delineated. A trail of dark hair disappearing into the waistband of low-slung cutoffs.

Wow.

Yes, Amber could see why Rochelle would think the Aces slugger would make the ideal fling. Not only did he exude animal sex appeal, he would also probably be on a plane in a day or two, safely gone from her life without doing any major damage. But the man was pure fantasy material and way out of Amber's league. She needed someone a bit more obtainable to help her regain her mojo.

She did want to put to rest her ex-boyfriend's damning accusation that she had Freon running through her veins when they were in bed together. She'd halfway believed him, knowing she'd always made safe and practical choices in her love life.

No more. She'd recalled an interesting book she reviewed about understanding sexual attraction and had promptly ordered a copy as a personal guide this week. As a longtime book lover, she remained convinced the answers to all the world's problems could be found in books if one had the patience to research. Armed with *The Mating Season,* Amber would make her first foray into living more passionately. And, thanks to the delectable man toweling off fifty yards away on their shared stretch of beach, Amber didn't have to worry about any ice in her veins. Sure, she had as much chance of snagging a guy like that as she had of roping the moon, but her two-minute fantasy reel of the baseball phenom had done her a big favor. For the first time in months, she felt sexy. And sexually interested.

As she headed back inside the house with a secret smile on her face and a new swing in her hips, Amber thought she just might have the guts to leave the safety of the beach house for a night on the town after all.

1

THE LAST THING Heath Donovan wanted was to leave the house tonight.

He cursed the need as he parked his motorcycle among the thirty-odd mopeds the tourists favored outside The Lighthouse, a local tavern that still served food at this hour. Too bad it also functioned as a big-time watering hole that was packed every night of the week with people who might recognize him.

Locking up the bike, a 1961 Velocette Venom that he kept on Nantucket so he wouldn't be tempted to rack up the mileage, he bypassed the main entrance. Instead, he headed for the door that led to the take-out kitchen, hoping he could get in and out without anyone noticing him. He had hobnobbed enough in his years as a player. As the Boston Aces' new manager, he preferred a lower profile, especially the day after a highly publicized game where he'd gotten tossed for supporting his catcher in a spat with the home plate ump.

Lowering the brim of his Patriots hat to help hide his

well-known mug, Heath opened the door to the building. The scent of barbecue and eighties rock music spilled out along with the dull glow of neon lights. The converted saltbox house was covered in gray cedar and perched at the water's edge near a decorative miniature lighthouse. But the picturesque New England vibe ended there. The place had been gutted to fit pool tables and jukeboxes, picnic tables and a dance floor. Tonight, the party overflowed onto the beach where the weekend bonfire would culminate in a midnight clambake.

He took his place in the waiting area—a backroom where they'd installed an extra bar and big-screen TVs for the take-out crowd. Heath wondered if the brunette he'd seen on his next-door neighbor's balcony would be here tonight. Unlike the downtown area of Nantucket, Great Point didn't have many choices for a night out. Would he catch sight of her white sundress in the crush?

Not that he planned to act on the rogue attraction that had washed over him like a wave off the sound. Right now, he needed to focus on plotting his way back into the administration's good graces if he wanted to keep the manager gig he'd worked his ass off to snag.

"Takeout for Jones." Heath called out the fake name to the woman behind the counter, the multipierced, purple-haired daughter of the guy who ran the place. He'd seen her here plenty of times before and knew she wouldn't recognize him—or the alias—since her eyes were always glued to the bouncer in the main bar.

The lady bartender gave Heath a nod, never glancing

twice at his face and making it easy for him to keep his cover. Leaving him to stare at the TV just in time to see highlight film of his ejection from last night's game.

He cursed under his breath, pissed all over again to see the pitch that extended the outside corner by two city blocks. And even more pissed to remember that if he wanted to stay in the majors as a manager, he couldn't champion all his players' causes. He backed away from the bar to wait until they called him, sticking to the shadows at the back of the room.

He didn't see the woman with her nose buried in a paperback book until he almost flattened her.

"Whoa!" She stumbled sideways, her hand reaching for him reflexively to regain her balance.

"Sorry," he muttered, keeping his head down, trying to stay out of the lights to avoid the hoopla that public recognition caused these days. He'd told the front office he would stay out of sight on his forced two-day leave from the ballpark—a bonus slap from the team's powers that be following the one-game suspension.

But the sight of a white sundress grazing tanned knees forced his head up in spite of himself.

It was the woman who'd been watching him from his neighbor's balcony. The image of the setting sun piercing her thin skirt to outline the shape of her legs had been the solitary high point in the past twenty-four hours from hell.

Not so long ago, he would have welcomed feminine distraction. Hell, there'd been a time when he would have thought nothing of introducing himself then and there and letting his star power do the hard work for him. But he couldn't think like some airheaded celebrity slugger when he was back at the bottom in his career, fighting for a slot he wanted to keep more than anything.

"It's okay." She released him quickly and straightened the neck of her dress's halter top, a sweetly modest gesture that stoked an unwanted attraction. "My friends always tell me I need to read less and live more." She gave the book in her hand a rueful wave and stuffed it in her purse.

"The Mating Season?" Curiosity got the better of him as he spied the title on the volume. He tilted his head to one side to read the cover that remained visible in the top of her denim drawstring bag. "'The primal dance of ancient gender politics'?"

Not exactly your everyday average light reading material. But definitely intriguing. And unlike the women who'd collided with him on purpose in bars over the years, he knew damn well that hadn't been this woman's intent. He'd been the one who'd run into her.

"This is by Madeline Watson-Turner. Great title, isn't it?" She seemed sincere, missing his cynicism as she passed him the volume. "The book came out a few years ago, but it's a great survey of human behavior. I find it interesting reading in light of, you know, the bar scene."

She gestured to the dance floor where couples now two-stepped to a country tune as a big, blue moon-shaped disco ball descended from the ceiling.

Heath didn't need to look around to know what she

referred to, however. He'd been a player in the so-called mating season plenty of times. Women flirted and primped, circling the room for the men that appealed to them most. Guys flexed muscles while doing innocuous things such as carrying a round of beers or setting up a shot at the pool table. All around them, men and women sent a hundred signals to each other in pursuit of that basic human need for intimacy.

"I think I recognize you from the beach earlier today." He figured he would give her the chance to 'fess up if she knew his identity. If she was a groupie—someone who'd put herself in his path on purpose because of his connection to baseball—he'd rather know now before he thought about her legs in a sundress any longer. "Any chance you're renting the house next to mine a few miles down the Point?"

Nodding, she peered over his shoulder as if looking for a way out of the conversation. What was up with that? She hadn't been nearly this distracted that afternoon when she'd been watching him from the porch of the house next door.

"That was me," she admitted. "I was long overdue for some R & R."

"Jones," the bartender called into the tinny public address system that alerted take-out customers when their orders were ready.

Damn. He wouldn't have minded standing here another minute or two to hear the brunette's name or find out why she was reading about the pickup scene while the rest of the bar-goers got on with the business of hooking up. Was she actively on the prowl tonight? A part of him really hated that idea. Something about her crisp white dress and bringing a book to a bar made her seem far too innocent to play that game.

"That's my order." He handed her book back as he nodded toward the front counter. "Guess my wings are ready."

She smiled as she again tucked the volume inside her bag.

"No sense letting good food get cold." She winked. "Enjoy your dinner."

Without another word, she disappeared into the crowd, weaving her way through the throng toward the back door that led outside.

Heading home? Or did she simply hope to find better light for reading at one of the outdoor picnic tables?

And had she recognized him and his connection to baseball? He seriously doubted it. If she had known who he was, she did a damn good job of acting as if his fame were no big deal—as if *he* were no big deal.

Because she wasn't the least bit impressed by fame? Or because she'd never opened the local sports section? He had to admit she had him curious. And not just because he remembered the exact shape of her legs from that sunset illumination of her dress earlier. In spite of his self-imposed moratorium on dating—or maybe because of it—he found himself drawn to the book-reading brunette.

"Jones, your order is ready." The voice on the PA system sounded more impatient now.

Between the woman at the counter's surly attitude and the sundress siren blowing him off without a backward glance, Heath realized he felt like a normal guy for a change. He blended into the background, just like he'd wanted.

As his eyes followed the path the brunette had taken, he found the idea of taking his wings home to devour in silence didn't hold quite the same appeal as it had an hour ago.

Stalking through the crowd toward the bar, he picked up his food. But by the time he had the bag in hand, he'd already made up his mind that he couldn't leave the bar until he satisfied his curiosity about the woman. When was the last time any female had conversed about a book with him? Hell, it'd been a long time since anyone had talked to him as if he knew anything about a topic outside of baseball. Besides, she was staying in the house next to his.

Even if he didn't have any intention of hitting on her, the least he could do was offer her a ride home.

AMBER WAS MORE THAN a little surprised to see her big league third baseman headed her way. After all, she rarely ever attracted anyone but sweetly nerdy types. A celebrated athlete pulling down millions a year was not even a remote possibility. But he approached her now, winding through the throng of beach volleyball players and couples staking out places around a bonfire near the water.

She had headed out here to snag some fresh air before

she made her first-ever move on some hapless studly type as part of her plan to be more emotionally daring. Well, that and she also hoped the darkness outside the bar would help ease her nervousness about approaching a stranger strictly to hit on him. Somehow the dark lent a sense of anonymity to the whole nerve-racking business. She'd found a spot at a picnic table at the edge of the action where she could people-watch and plot her next move.

But the sight of Rochelle's megahot neighbor walking toward her saved her from having to flirt with some random stranger for a little while longer. Which was not only utterly unexpected, it was welcome news. She'd felt an odd connection with the star player when he'd bumped into her, when he'd held her steady with strong, warm hands. Crazy, yes. Improbable, definitely.

That didn't stop the way her eyes found his in a crowd while the rest of the world faded to insignificance.

Of course, that only meant *he* was magnetic as hell. She had no reason to feel as if the moment was full of destiny as he ambled his gorgeous self closer to her. She purposely hadn't tried to hone her flirting skills on him because he must be highly sought after by women who were a whole lot better than her at this dating business. Maybe she was just damned glad to see him because now she could relax.

Since the ballplayer wasn't a dating prospect, she could let her guard down and be herself around him.

"According to my book—" she patted the volume

resting in her purse pocket "—you should move closer to the center of action if you're hoping to meet people."

Not that she necessarily wanted to watch him hooking up with any of the endlessly tall, cool blondes that seemed to populate Nantucket this weekend. But it was second nature to share the tidbits she'd picked up about dating from the book.

As a book reviewer, she frequently read about life instead of living it. At first, the tactic had been a brilliant way to save herself from a tumultuous childhood, holding her mom's hand between husbands who let her down. But at the age of twenty-eight, Amber knew her old standby of finding life's answers in a library wasn't exactly a healthy practice.

The ballplayer paused in front of her picnic table, empty save her. Most of the bar patrons were dancing—either inside or out—or playing beach games such as bocce and horseshoes near the water. Torches ringed the property, while a few strands of Christmas lights illuminated walkways and the gazebo down by a small pier.

He deposited a paper take-out bag on the end of the table and then—surprise—*two* bottles of beer.

"What makes you think I need tips from a book?" He sat down, uninvited but not unwelcome.

It gave her the chance to peruse him at length close-up. And, man, what a treat it was to ogle a handsome male from such an intimate distance. His knee brushed hers under the table, the denim rough against her bare leg.

She appreciated the casualness that kept her from getting nervous around him. Or worse, prickly. Sometimes when she liked a guy, her defenses turned into force fields worthy of a Starfleet ship.

"Oh, I don't know. I guess because you barrel through the place knocking women down before they know what hit them—"

"I hardly knocked you down." He set a longneck closer to her and moved his aside so he could open the box full of chicken wings with a side of ribs. "But in an effort to make it up to you, I've brought you dinner."

He picked up his beer bottle and clinked the side gently against hers where the brew still sat on the table.

"To chance encounters that don't have a damn thing to do with the mating season," he offered as a toast.

Charmed, she lifted the cold bottle and clinked it back.

"Cheers." Tipping the glass to her lips, she watched him do the same, her heartbeat stuttering at his warm regard.

She knew better than to pay attention to good looks— she'd trained that instinct out of herself at an early age, realizing even in high school that she had more fun hanging out with guys who could look beneath the surface. Still, here was the baseball hero, looking her right in the eye and seeming to like what he saw just fine.

"I'm Heath, by the way." He slid a paper plate across the table with a half-dozen wings. "Dig in."

Heath? Amber couldn't recall the name of the ballplayer, but she'd thought it was something more Hispanic sounding than Heath. She wasn't sure if Heath was part of the alias—as "Jones" so obviously had been—or if she'd gotten mixed up about the name Rochelle had mentioned. She'd never paid any attention to professional sports.

"Amber Nichols, book reviewer extraordinaire," she returned, telling herself it didn't matter either way since she hadn't expected him to be honest with her. Men in bars lied all the time. Even *The Mating Season* said so. "I've already eaten, but thanks for the beer."

She took another sip, savoring the icy flavor of a Boston microbrew while she watched him devour his first two wings.

"I figured if I bought you a drink maybe you'd fill me in on why you brought a book to a bar on a Friday night. But I guess I have my answer. You're writing a book review?"

The outdoor speakers blared a reggae tune while a new volleyball game got under way and the previous rivals paired off to walk on the beach. Amber realized her pool of dating prospects was dwindling, but with Heath sitting across from her, it was hard to care. He could seriously turn a woman's head.

"It's a long overdue case of reading for pleasure." She hadn't picked up a book of her own choosing in months.

He paused in his methodical demolishing of the food.

"If you're hanging out in a meat market like this, it seems like you could observe all you need to about—what was it?—the 'ancient dance of gender politics' from a firsthand perspective. Why be here and use the time to read?"

"Great question," she admitted, drawn to the natural inquisitiveness in his eyes that didn't seem like a put-on. "And I'm honestly not sure if it's because I'm too much of a chicken to face a bar crowd while I'm alone, or because I need a great deal of remedial help playing the pickup game."

She'd decided to be sincere with him since he was just being friendly.

A chicken wing fell from his fingers and he appeared surprised for a moment before he grinned and shook his head.

"It was a serious question."

Confused, she frowned.

"It was a serious answer."

He leaned back in his seat and angled his head to see under the table. Then, straightening, he looked her in the eye again.

"With legs like that, I find it tough to believe you don't rake in your fair share of male attention." He turned his gaze back to his dinner.

Flustered and half wishing she could consult her book for advice on what a guy like Heath might want from this kind of conversation with a woman of her tepid outward charm, Amber tensed.

"Now who's not being serious?" She knew very well her legs were nothing to write home about. The temptation to open up *The Mating Season* and reread the chapter "Liars, Posers and Pickup Artists" made her fingers itch. "I'm only here because I need to force myself to be more social."

His eyebrows lifted in unison, perhaps reacting to the surliness that had crept into her tone.

"Okay, *that* I believe. Are you always this defensive?"

"Actually, I'm being amazingly friendly toward you." When was the last time she'd let a stranger buy her a drink, let alone sit down and make himself at home at her table at an overcrowded nightclub? "I think it's because I'm certain you have no interest in me."

Heath balled up the paper plate and stuffed it inside the empty sack before sending the bag sailing in a neat hook shot into a nearby trash can.

"Well, Amber, I guess that just proves you can't learn everything you need to know from books because I'm more than interested." He lowered his voice and the brim of his ball cap as a group of women sat down at a table right next to theirs. "I'm flat-out attracted and hoping you'll let me take you home."

2

AMBER'S JAW DROPPED in an expression that was downright priceless. Had the male population become so blinded by a generation of silicone-enhanced females that they didn't recognize a truly hot version of the real thing?

He couldn't think of any other reason why Amber Nichols would have gotten this far in life without having a better awareness of her own appeal.

"Isn't that moving a little fast?" Her hand strayed to her purse, where that book of hers stuck out of an outside pocket. She ran an unvarnished nail along the closed pages, creating a soft zipping noise.

Heath couldn't remember ever having a conversation like this one. He'd been on the receiving end of big-time female attention from the time he was an All-State baseball player as a ninth grader on the varsity team. As a major leaguer, he'd had women stalk him, flash him and bribe the elevator guy in his building to get close to him. Not once in all that time had a woman questioned his technique.

"I don't know," he deadpanned. "Should we check the book?"

For a moment, she bit her lip and he wondered if she was honestly tempted. He half regretted teasing her.

"Make fun if you want, but I'm a little out of my element here." She stood abruptly, putting her purse strap over her shoulder and leaving the beer on the table. "Thanks for the drink, but I think I'll be heading home."

Strike. Out.

She couldn't have made the call any more clearly if she'd been sporting a blue shirt and a chest protector. Her long, dark braid whipped over her shoulder to trail obediently behind her as she walked away from him for the second time that night.

And for the second time, he realized he didn't want her to go.

Something about uptight, blind-to-her-own-appeal Amber Nichols made him want to turn her around and show her the time of her life. It seemed like a truly ill-timed impulse given the state of his slipping career status and his well-under-.500 ball club.

But look where all his intense focus on the team had gotten him. Booted out of the ballpark for two days until he could rein in his mouth and his temper on the field.

What if Ms. Serious who didn't know his famous name was just the ticket to a major attitude adjustment for him? He'd been so determined to set women aside this year. What if all the pent-up anger and stress stemmed from a lack of that basic release? Maybe he really needed the mood-altering benefits of a rollicking good time with a woman who was about as far from a clingy groupie as he could possibly get.

His feet were already making tracks to follow her while his brain slowly caught up. This was a good idea.

Instead of two days of reinventing his losing team, he'd have two days of Amber. Two days of mouthwatering legs. Two days of teasing her about her choice of reading material while showing her how sexy she really was.

Assuming he had any idea how to seduce a woman. The very real possibility that he'd only ever gotten laid because of his bat speed gave him pause.

"Amber." He caught up with her in the parking lot as she searched the long row of mopeds. "Sorry to give you such a hard time back there. I'm a wiseass, but sometimes it strays more toward pain in the ass."

She nodded, hardly looking at him.

"It's okay. I'm very uppity," she admitted, not sounding overly concerned about it. "Apparently I'm also very forgetful as I have no idea which one of these is my rental."

His eyes followed hers down the row of scooters, half of which were the exact same make, model and color. Even the helmets were identical since the local dealership issued the same basic gear to everyone.

"Well, I offered to drive you home earlier since you're

staying at the beach house right next to mine. The offer still stands."

She straightened from her examination of the vehicles.

"You said you wanted to take me *home*." She pursed her mouth in a thoughtful little frown and he wondered what her lips would taste like if he nibbled on one. They looked slick and glossy, and he bet they smelled good, too. "I thought you meant you wanted to…"

He wondered if she was blushing as her words trailed off. He almost wouldn't be surprised. She was an interesting mix of fresh honesty and disarming sweetness. He all around liked Amber Nichols.

"I do. That is, you didn't misunderstand." He closed the distance between them, the scent of the ocean and the bonfire filling the air. "I issued a purposely ambiguous invitation, thinking I'd be happy if you took me up on it no matter how you interpreted it."

Her fist tightened on the key in her hand, her dark braid slithering over one bare shoulder as she straightened.

"So you *did* proposition me?" She sounded surprised.

"I did." He gestured toward his classic British motorcycle parked between the scooters and the Jeeps. "But you deserve a much better proposition than that. You can listen to my pitch on the way home and if you don't like it, I'll drop you at your doorstep—no harm, no foul."

"I don't think I'm going to be able to hear a proposition if I ride on that thing." She lifted one eyebrow, her expression skeptical.

He thought of all the women he'd known who would slither suggestively all over that bike for the chance to ride with him. And damn, but wasn't it different to be the one doing the convincing for a change?

"So technically, you might have to hear the pros and cons on your front porch instead of on the highway." He snagged a generic helmet off the nearest scooter and handed it to her. "Here. Put this on. No matter whose it is, there are enough here for everyone since you wore one."

She hesitated, peering back over her shoulder at the beach party kicking into high gear with the scent of the clambake and a vintage Lynyrd Skynyrd tune drifting on the breeze.

Heath dug for the last bit of persuasive ammo he could think of without touching her.

"I thought you wanted to read less and live more?" He parroted her words from earlier when he'd run into her.

Apparently, she was committed to that bit of wisdom because the prompt worked like a charm. She snatched the helmet from him and strapped it in place.

"You're on."

He didn't bother to hide a grin as he secured his own helmet and fired up the engine. She never hesitated when it came time to straddle the bike in her dress. With modesty and determination, she managed the trick without flashing him.

A damn shame.

"Ready?" he asked, looking forward to the moment when she realized she'd need to wrap herself around him.

As it was, she sat with her knees grazing his thighs, but the fun stopped there.

"I think so?" The rising inflection suggested she'd quite possibly never ridden a motorcycle.

"Hold on to me." The words came out rougher than he'd intended. Not that he was frustrated. If anything, he was more eager than he would have imagined to have her touch him.

There was a light brush of fingertips along his upper back.

"Uh, lower." His skin tightened with the myriad of implications in that one simple word.

Her touch vanished briefly, then reappeared at his waist. She slid her arms around him, her breasts pressed against his back.

"I'm beginning to think you had an ulterior motive in wanting to give me a ride."

He blinked to clear his mind of the wicked double entendres he'd begun to hear in their every exchange. She had his pulse fired up so hard he couldn't think straight.

"Is that right?"

She tucked her chin against his shoulder as he backed out of the parking spot and pulled onto the highway.

"I think you knew all along the persuasive measures

were going to start on the way home, even if we weren't speaking."

She'd seen straight through him. But fortunately, she didn't sound annoyed about it. If anything, she just might be warming up to the idea of spending the night with him if the pebble-hard peaks of her breasts against his back were any indication.

No matter that his ball club was at the bottom of their division and the team owner was gunning for his ass. At this moment, everything felt right in his world.

AMBER WORRIED THAT HER brain had shut off right about the time her libido kicked into high gear.

Maybe that was why she'd always avoided situations like this.

She could never remember feeling so sexually edgy that she was about to come out of her skin.

Was it because of the element of daring involved with flirting with a stranger? The frank masculine appeal of a man who'd turned her on physically with just one look even before she'd arrived at the bar that night?

Or could it be the raw stimulation of having her thighs wrapped around Heath with nothing but a layer of cotton sundress and whisper-thin silk panties to separate her from the rough denim of his jeans?

No doubt it was a potent combination of all of the above. He revved the engine faster on a straightaway that cut through a patch of trees, casting them in even more shadows without the glow of the moon. She tightened her hold on his waist, her hands splayed against the rigid muscles of his abs.

And, heaven help her, she couldn't even think about words such as *rigid* without getting all hot and bothered. Which brought her to yet another reason for her turned-on condition. Heath had put the whole notion of sleeping together into her brain, the possibility teasing her thoughts at every turn until she could barely think at all. She could only feel.

The motor hummed a conspiratorial vibration between her legs, a ridiculously erotic stimulation that reminded her of sex. Well, right now, everything seemed to remind her of sex.

She closed her eyes to shut out the inviting sight of Heath's V-shaped back tapering into narrow hips. But that only made the scent of his skin beneath his shirt more tempting. Amazing how as soon as you deprived one of your senses, the others all became more acute.

What am I doing?

It was quite possibly the last rational plea of her reasonable mind, so accustomed to being in total control. She didn't want to be the half-witted woman whose body was washed up on the beach the next morning because she went home with a stranger.

But Heath wasn't a stranger. He was a well-known public figure who would be risking his million-dollar contract if he got into trouble with the law. Plus, Rochelle knew Heath and knew Amber was with him. Amber had texted her friend while Heath was starting up the bike before she left.

Besides, he'd never once flaunted his star status to impress her. He could have used that to try to woo her in some smarmy pickup, but he hadn't even mentioned it. He seemed like a regular guy. A really hot regular guy.

Bottom line, Amber had come to the beach for just this kind of thing—to prove she could have a passionate, hot encounter without overthinking the whole thing. She wasn't a cold fish. She didn't have to plan every second of her life, which had been another one of Brent's accusations before he left.

It would be okay to let go of reason for a few hours. Maybe even all night. Heath was charming. Forthright. Sexy. Best of all, he was only interested in the here and now. She didn't have to worry about confusing, emotionally draining entanglements.

He might even be gone before she woke up in the morning.

What could one night with him possibly hurt?

She'd thought so long about it that she didn't realize they were home until Heath rolled the bike to a stop and flicked off the engine.

Suddenly, she sat in the dark chill of the cooling night air, clinging to his back for dear life for no other reason than that he felt so good.

So warm. So fiercely masculine.

"Amber?"

His voice scratched over her senses, satisfying an itch and somehow heightening them at the same time.

"Mmm?" She told herself to let go of him, but her hands wouldn't obey.

The only response she got from her fingers was a slight flex against his abs, raking gently along the hard muscle there.

"We're home." He placed a warm palm against the outside of her bare thigh where her dress had hiked up to straddle the bike.

Ooh.

The broad splay of his fingers awakened her senses to even more sensual possibilities. What might those hands accomplish if given free rein over her body tonight?

She felt her nipples bead even harder against his back. The impulse to rub herself against him like a cat gripped her so forcefully she could barely resist it.

"I'm aware of that." With an effort, she unlinked her hands from his waist and reached up to unfasten her helmet. "Guess I got a little too comfortable."

Hooking the helmet on the back of the bike, she stood. Her body protested the loss of his and she wondered if her reaction to him was so fierce because she'd denied herself this kind of outlet her whole life.

Wasn't she the woman who chose her dates intellectually? Based on common interests? That had always seemed so smart and so much safer than dating random guys just because they looked good. But maybe she really had missed some important dating knowledge by denying herself the occasional—er—booty call?

"Comfortable?" Heath was off the bike and standing

inches in front of her before she could catch her breath. "Is that what we were feeling the whole way home?"

She wondered how he knew what she felt. His dark, intent stare sure looked as if he had full knowledge of her riotous impulses. Could he honestly be feeling all those same things?

Her legs wobbled unsteadily beneath her. She hadn't felt so boy-crazy since her first high-school dance.

"Maybe *comfortable* wasn't quite the word I was looking for. Thank you for the ride."

She had no idea how to go about inviting him inside, probably because she'd never tried to make a move on a guy so early in a relationship. But damn it, she didn't want a relationship. She wanted mindless forgetting.

She wanted to feel hot and sexy and passionate. And her every tingling feminine instinct told her she could feel that way with Heath.

"You sound so formal," he teased, smiling. "I thought we got past that stage on the ride home."

Amen. But she didn't say that. Clearing her throat, Amber called up all her courage.

"Would you like to come in?" At some point during the asking she realized she was shaking inside—and a little on the outside, too.

Damn Brent for stealing her confidence and making her doubt herself.

Heath peered over one shoulder toward Rochelle's beach house.

"Actually, I'm afraid I won't be able to keep my hands off you once I cross that threshold." He made it a friendly warning, but the tense set to his shoulders told her he might not be kidding. "I'd rather not go in unless I'm sure I'll be staying all night."

In the old days—her pre-Brent days—she would have thought Heath's statement was coming on too strong. Right now, she liked the idea that he wanted her.

"I'm not sure—" she started, licking her lips since the words had dried up in her throat.

The breeze off the water blew her skirt lightly against her legs; the scent of the sea and Heath's aftershave wove around her.

"That's where the conversation comes in, remember?" He slipped a hand around her elbow and guided her toward the balcony where she'd stood a few hours earlier and ogled him shamelessly.

Back then, she'd been content to simply let the sight of a handsome man rev her snoozing libido. She'd never thought she would actually be returning here with him tonight.

"You're really going to try to sell me on spending the night with you?" She couldn't imagine he did that very often. Major League Baseball players had their pick of women at all times, right?

Her small kitten heels sank in the sand with each step as she followed him across the driveway and up the steps to the balcony. Once there, he wasted no time backing her onto the fat green cushions of the porch glider. He dropped down to the seat beside her, close but no longer touching.

He seemed respectful like that, despite his frank way

of speaking. Amber thought Rochelle had said he was a young player, but Heath had a definite maturity about him. He obviously knew not to crowd her.

Now, he studied her in the moonlight, the soft white glow surrounding them in a bubble of privacy while the ocean waves rolled a relentless rhythm nearby. Cool sea spray carried on the breeze, coating her skin in a mist that made her shiver.

"Amber, I'm going to be honest with you." He angled his body between hers and the sea, effectively sheltering her from both the wind and the mist.

"I would hope so." She smoothed her skirt over her legs, the hem just barely reaching her knee. "I'm contemplating a fun fling, not a smarmy affair based on lies." Even as she said it, a horrible thought formed. "You're not married, are you?"

She figured Rochelle would have known, but what if her friend hadn't been aware of all the facts?

"Divorced for three years, actually," Heath clarified. "I'm not marriage material by a long stretch. In fact, I'm not even good dating material."

"I'm not looking for dating," she said. "God, that sounds tawdry, doesn't it? I'm sure this is supposed to be a lot less awkward. But I've never considered sleeping with someone just for—you know—fun."

Heath shook his head, a slow grin stealing over his mouth. What would it feel like to have those lips on hers?

"You're too much, Amber." He brushed his fingers along the side of her cheek, his thumb straying beneath her lower lip. "It's a good thing I got you out of The Lighthouse before you tried out your *Mating Season* techniques on the unsuspecting male population."

"You think I would have been a colossal failure, don't you?" She marveled at the way his light stroke could elicit a swirl of pleasure deep inside her, far from the point of contact.

How did he do that?

"I'm glad you weren't wasted on someone who wouldn't have appreciated you as much as I will." He lifted his thumb a millimeter or two, just enough to land on the plump center of her lower lip.

Somehow, he'd turned the most gentle of touches into something wildly erotic. Or had she built it into something carnal with her wayward imaginings?

"It's nice to be appreciated," she admitted, straining to maintain eye contact when her lids wanted to fall closed.

What would happen if she just gave in to what she wanted?

"I can do a lot better than this," he promised, his voice soft next to her ear, making her realize her eyes must have closed long enough that she hadn't seen him lean near.

His whisper made the back of her neck tingle.

"I'd like to see you try." She couldn't begin to imagine what pleasurable havoc he might wreak if she committed herself to this night with him.

"Then what's stopping you from saying yes?" His

hand strayed lower, his fingers dipping beneath her hair while his thumb tipped her chin up.

Their eyes met for a long moment and she wondered which of her many fears to list. That things would be awkward between them in the morning? That her relationship instincts would kick in tomorrow and she'd mess up the fling by falling for him? She knew he was a wildly inappropriate choice for her heart.

But she didn't say any of that. Without thinking, she voiced her biggest worry.

"I'm afraid of being a sexual disappointment."

3

OF ALL THE THINGS Heath thought he might hear regarding Amber's reservation, a fear of disappointing him never would have crossed his radar.

He had to stop himself from saying "What?" emphasized with a raised voice and a few audible exclamation marks, even though that was his internal reaction. From the tentative note in her tone the first time, he guessed she wouldn't want to repeat the declaration.

So, smothering the urge to express disbelief and a healthy amount of outrage at whoever had put that kind of notion in her head, he managed to keep his tone neutral.

"Any man who claims to be disappointed in you is an idiot who's too scared to admit he only disappoints himself." He knew he might be condemning someone she'd once cared for, but how could he let her worry about something like that? He had a quick image of the kind of guy who would take advantage of a relatively inexperienced woman by making her think crap sex was *her* fault. The mental picture forced him to take his hands off her since his fingers flexed into automatic fists.

"You think so?" She wrapped her arms around herself, her expression dubious.

"I know so with a thousand percent certainty." The urge to gather her up in his arms and take her inside pulled at him with new ferocity.

Before, he'd wanted her because she made him feel like a regular guy, as if his wealth and fame didn't matter one bit. They'd just been two people attracted at the most basic level.

Now, he also wanted to prove to her beyond all doubt that she had the power to turn a man inside out with wanting her.

"There's no such thing as thousand percent certainty." The worry had faded from her voice as she flicked at the hem of her dress.

"There is in this case." He unclenched his fists now, determined that the best way to take revenge on the jerk who'd hurt her was to provide her with the most excellent sex of her life. Laying his palm over her hand where it sat on her knee, he let his touch speak for him. "Why don't you let me prove it to you?"

Her big, dark eyes, guarded but curious, met his in the moonlight. They definitely had a connection and he was more than happy to exploit it for their mutual benefit. She might not know how good it could be between them, but he did.

So, operating on instinct, he allowed two fingers to stray off the fabric of her skirt to brush her bare knee.

Higher.

He remembered how responsive she'd been on the back of his bike. How she'd pressed herself against him once she'd given in and put her arms around him. He used that knowledge now to shamelessly coax the answer he wanted to hear.

"You're very persuasive," she admitted, her voice catching on a breathy note that teased his senses like a caress.

"Is that a yes?" Taking no chances, he pressed his advantage by lowering his mouth to hers.

Gently, he kissed her. Carefully, he kept the contact light so that he could walk away if she chose not to move forward.

He hadn't counted on her reaction.

She didn't sit still for the kiss. The tender meeting of mouths intended to seal the deal didn't remain chaste for long. Later, he would think to himself that the kiss had been like a spark in a dry forest. Instantly, everything took flame.

Amber's arms were around his neck, her soft skin and faint fragrance surrounding him. Her hips twisted toward his, her thigh pressed against his leg.

And her breasts...the sudden feel of her high, firm curves thrust to his chest brought on a blood rush that left him dizzy.

"That's a yes," he growled against her lips, breaking

the kiss long enough to speak. "Where's the key to the house?"

"In my purse." She had sidled into his lap as if she belonged there, her fingers twining through his hair. "Hurry."

He was still reeling from the sensual onslaught. "We have all night," he assured her, needing to catch his breath before he untied the halter top of her dress while they were still outdoors. "There's no need to rush."

She wriggled and resituated herself on his lap, her hip nudging him at a crucial juncture that damn near undid him.

"I didn't feel in a rush either until you started talking about thousand percent certainty and put your hand on my thigh." She let go of his neck to pick up the purse he hadn't been able to find in the dark. Emerging with a key, she dropped it in his hand. "Now I'm all kinds of curious and more than a little excited about how this is going to turn out."

Apparently satisfied she'd done her part to get them inside the house, she returned her attention to his mouth. Nipping his lip, she smoothed the spot with a quick dart of her tongue.

A groan ripped through him, the sound vibrating in his ears and humming along his skin as he rose to stand with her in his arms. Fumbling with the key and trying like hell to avoid the temptation of sliding a hand up her skirt, Heath plowed through the door of the beach house.

He dropped the key on a counter of some kind and

toed the door shut with his boot. He walked slowly since he'd never been in the house before and he didn't want to ram into a piece of furniture with Amber in his arms.

"Which way?" he asked, arching away from her kiss long enough to obtain that vital piece of information.

"My room is at the top of the stairs. Through the living room on the right." She whispered even though they were alone in the darkened house. Moonlight poured in through a few windows where the shades hadn't been drawn, allowing him to make out the polished banister of a staircase. "But the living room is okay with me."

"Not a chance." He hastened his pace, hoping to hit the steps before she kissed him again and his brainpower diminished. "I'm not going to let you get distracted by a sofa spring in your back or rug burn on the knees. I made you a promise that we're going to have the time of our lives tonight, and that damn well means a mattress."

"Rug burn?"

He took the steps faster than most of his rookie players could have, even with Amber in his arms. Then again, it was having Amber in his arms that drove him to find the bedroom so fast.

"Nothing you need to worry about now," he assured her, maneuvering her through the doorframe with care so he didn't bump into anything.

The room faced the ocean. Moonlight spilled in through the open French doors while the vast blackness stretched out on the other side. A white spread on an old iron four-poster bed, one of the few pieces of furniture on the sprawl of gently worn hardwood, welcomed them.

He hesitated before reaching the mattress.

"There." She pointed, as if he couldn't see the bed for himself.

"Not yet." He figured he was the one carrying her, so he could choose where they landed. Positioning her just in front of the French doors, he set her on her feet. "I've been remembering all night the way your legs looked with the setting sun shining through that skirt earlier. I'm thinking I can re-create the visual if the moon is bright enough."

He stepped back to admire the view, the moonlight giving her a back glow like an angel in her white dress. And how damn poetic was that?

"You're crazy," she admonished, fidgeting her way out of her shoes, clearly uncomfortable in the spotlight.

"Maybe." He reached for the long rope of hair snaking down one shoulder and caught the end. "Can I unfasten this?"

He pulled at the elastic.

"Um, sure. But this isn't some kind of Cinderella deal where I let my hair down and suddenly I'm gorgeous."

Pulling the hair tie free, he slipped a finger into one loop after another, methodically untwining the hair as silky waves slithered over his palms.

"No 'suddenly' about it." She was naturally beautiful either way.

The process was deliciously slow, and he took his

time, enjoying the feel of her hair as it cloaked her shoulders.

She stepped closer, her eyes heavy-lidded.

"Only one knot left to unfasten," she whispered, pulling the long mane to one side of her neck and revealing the tie of her halter top.

His pulse stuttered and sped up. How had he gotten so fortunate as to run into this woman tonight? A woman who didn't know about his career and didn't care what he did for a living. She hadn't even asked.

Unable to keep his distance any longer, he hauled her up against him. Easing the knot in her dress, he undid the soft cotton until the triangles of fabric covering her breasts loosened and fell free.

But the feel of her pressed up against him didn't compare with the sexy gasp from her lips. The sound tripped down his spine like a lover's fingertip.

"No more knots." He smoothed his hands down her bare shoulders, absorbing her shiver as he bent to kiss her neck.

"Good." She arched back enough to yank his shirt hem up and splay a hand along his bare stomach. "That means no more delays. No more waiting."

He had to admit it was tougher to be on the receiving end of sensual touches than to be the giver. Her fingers gliding just below the waist of his jeans couldn't have been more potent if she'd been stroking his shaft.

Heat blazed up his chest in spite of the cool breeze blowing in the window.

"I'd do a better job delivering on all those promises I

made if you let me take my time." Even now, his hands shook with the need to hold back. It had been a hell of a long time since he'd been with a woman.

And ah damn, but he was feeling every one of those months—no, a year now—as Amber peeled off his shirt and stepped out of her dress.

Wow, she was an eyeful.

A barely there lace strapless bra matched white bikini bottoms. A thin silver chain looped around her waist and dangled three dark blue gemstones just beneath her belly button.

"It's because of those damn promises that I'm in a hurry," she argued with whispered urgency as she brushed kisses along his jaw. "I have bad memories to live down, remember?"

AMBER KNEW HEATH MUST have recalled her predicament, her wish to make sure she wasn't sexually deficient.

His touch went from reverent to mind-blowingly commanding. He lifted her off her feet and carried her to the bed, her unbound hair trapped between their bodies as he laid her on the chenille bedspread.

"Kiss me," he ordered, his tone warning that he wouldn't tolerate an argument.

Obediently, she arched against him, savoring the rough scrape of his whiskers against her cheek and the press of his thigh between hers. He was too good to be true. Too delicious for words.

She'd never imagined she could be the kind of woman

who would find so much satisfaction in the physical, but right now she was a mass of throbbing want. How had she gone through life for twenty-eight years without ever seeking this kind of pleasure?

"Stop thinking," he muttered between kisses, breaking away from her mouth to lick his way down her neck.

His hot breath against her skin made her writhe against the mattress, which only succeeded in rubbing her thighs against his. She wondered if a woman could explode from desire.

"How do you know I'm thinking?" She hadn't been doing much of that. "I've mostly been panting and moaning and that sort of thing."

She tried to unfasten his jeans, but her fingers hummed with some kind of trembly energy as if she'd stuck her hand in a light socket.

"You weren't moaning," he assured her, circling a nipple with his tongue right through the lace of her bra. "I would have heard you."

She moaned. And not just for effect.

"That feels—" She couldn't explain it since she moaned again.

"That's more like it." He tugged down one lace cup with his teeth. Then he unveiled the other the same way.

"What else can I do?" She didn't want to let him take the lead so much that tomorrow he would look back and think she'd been a failure in the sack. Not after what Brent had said to her. "How can I help?"

He lifted his gaze from her breasts for a moment, and the look she saw there sent a peculiar shiver along the back of her neck. Intense and determined, he didn't have the appearance of a young rookie sowing his wild oats with women far and wide. Just then, he had the hell-bent will of a man who could move mountains if he so chose.

"You can think about me." He took her hand in his and guided it to his shorts where an impressive bulge awaited her. "Only me. And how much I want you."

It was a sexy thing to say. It was also a beautiful thing to say to ease the last of her fears.

And just then, Amber had a taste of the dangers of sleeping with someone just for fun. Because with that simple statement, Heath had touched her heart no matter how much she wanted this to be uncomplicated.

But then, he palmed the throbbing place between her legs, applying sinfully delicious pressure where she wanted it most. Raw hunger edged out emotion and fears. She couldn't hold back the gasps and sighs as he worked the most sensitive places until she was slick with desire.

She had just enough sense to be sure he found a condom from somewhere before she allowed herself to become utterly mindless at his touch. Her panties disappeared around the same time he stripped off the rest of his clothes. The room became a sultry blur of body heat and ocean breeze, their limbs tangling in a teasing dance until at last he entered her.

Her nails bit into his skin at the same time her teeth

nipped her lower lip. She'd never felt anything like what she felt with Heath. She lost herself in him, in this. Mindless with the sweetness of it all, she realized she shouldn't have to think so hard about sex. It could just happen. And be wonderful.

Her heartbeat thundered like a storm coming in off the water. An urgent fire built in her blood. She twisted her head back and forth against the pillow as he drove into her again and again. Slow, then fast. Slow again.

Her breaths came so quick she couldn't catch them. Her legs wound around him tight, clutching him hard and squeezing him to her as he found a spot that turned her into a crazy woman.

Release crashed through her so forcefully and for so long she thought it would never end. Waves of pleasure squeezed her insides, wringing every last sweet spasm from her until Heath joined her. Feeling his release was almost as gratifying as the amazing orgasm he'd given her. Knowing she'd satisfied him—this amazing, sexy, thoughtful man who could have his pick of women—made her glow with happiness, if only for a little while.

Tomorrow, she would think about how to say goodbye to him. How to forget the way he'd touched her heart even as he touched her body. But for tonight, she planned to cling to her third baseman for all he was worth, taking every ounce of pleasure she could find until the sun rose.

When she finally caught her breath, she kissed his shoulder and combed her hair off his chest.

"So tell me, slugger, how does it feel to hit one out of the park?"

4

THE WORDS KNIFED through Heath's euphoria like a one-hundred-mile-per-hour fastball coming at a man without a glove.

"What?" His hands slid away from Amber's shoulders, confusion fogging his brain.

Could it be a coincidence that she used a sports metaphor?

"You know." She gestured meaningfully toward their bodies where their legs were still entwined. "I don't know if you've got sexual superpowers or if that's normal for you, but...wow."

She smiled and his euphoria returned, relaxing his tense shoulders. He didn't doubt for a minute it had been fantastic between them.

"Right." Closing his eyes, he leaned deeper into the pillow, thinking he was comfortable enough he might spend the whole night here. "When you said 'hit it out of the park,' I—"

"You thought I was going to quiz you about your

day job?" She reached behind her to tug a corner of the bedspread up over her shoulder.

Heath froze.

The blissed-out warmth he'd known a few moments ago dissipated.

"You knew who I was?" A lifetime of being sought after only for his wealth and fame gave the question more bite than he'd intended.

She must have heard it, because she quit tucking the spread around her and looked up at him. Her body tensed.

"Some big-deal third baseman, according to Rochelle. The friend who owns this house," she clarified. Then, as if to lighten the mood, she winked. "Why? Were you trying to keep it secret?"

He didn't know where to begin addressing that question. Had she targeted him from the minute she'd arrived? Or maybe she'd been content to meet some random player, clearly confusing him with Diego Estes. He didn't want to shuffle his view of her to accommodate that new information, far preferring his idea of her as sweet and awkward. Overtly brainy but quietly beautiful. But now, his whole perspective shifted.

"Oh, my God." Reaching for the bedspread again, she pulled it closer. "You really did want to keep it a secret."

The confusion in her voice didn't seem like an act. But damn. He'd been taken in by women who were only trying to get close to his job in the past. He wasn't in any position right now to read her motives.

He swiped his hand over his head, wishing he could wipe away the new ache that had started in his temples.

"It's no secret." Plenty of well-known personalities made trips to the islands off Cape Cod, so it was not as if he thought he was hiding. "But if you were trying to hook up with the third baseman, you got the wrong guy."

He was about as far from ladies' man Diego Estes as he could get. Grabbing his shirt, he got to his feet and pulled it on.

"I wasn't trying to *hook up* with anyone." Her voice was steely.

"What about *The Mating Season?*"

"Oh. Yes." That seemed to fluster her. "Well, I was trying to educate myself on the dating scene to help me meet people, but I certainly didn't set out to meet some big-deal ballplayer whose name means nothing to me anyway." She paused in the middle of the rant, sat up and yanked his socks out of his hand before he could put them on. "Wait a minute. Who are you if you don't play for the Aces?"

She looked so distressed at the idea he wasn't a major leaguer that it steeled any trace of regret at walking out on her. Memories of all the low-down tricks groupies had used to meet him came back with a vengeance—right down to the phone call a crazed lady fan had placed to his new wife, pretending to be his mistress. Anger burned hot in his gut as his brain lumped Amber into that category of tricksters.

Wrenching his socks back, he jammed them in his back pocket as he headed for the door.

"Instead of reading a book on how to meet guys, next time you ought to pick up a players' roster so you know who you're talking to." He paused to look at her, silhouetted against the bed with the moonlight as a backdrop. "I don't play for the Aces. I manage them."

Walking out of her bedroom, he didn't look back.

HEATH HAD BARELY returned home when his cell phone started ringing.

He knew it couldn't be Amber since she didn't have his number. Furthermore, she probably didn't want to speak to him any more than he did to her. He'd been a little harsher than he'd intended.

Pulling the phone from his pants pocket, he saw the caller ID. Of all the freaking luck, it was Diego Estes, the Aces' third baseman that Amber had mistaken him for.

"Estes, dude, it's almost two in the morning."

"Is it that late already?" the kid shouted over music blaring in the background and the noise of a few hundred other hardcore partying types. "Sorry about that. I just wondered if you've seen my iPod. I think I left it at your beach house."

Heath had walked straight into the living room and turned on the television to distract him from thinking about Amber and how he'd rather be oblivious and in her bed than wise to her maneuvering and alone in his place.

"No sign of it, but I'll leave a note for the cleaning people and see if they find it when they come in."

"You okay, Skip?" The kid seemed to have found a quieter corner of the bar or party or wherever he was because the pulsing bass had decreased in the background.

It still made Heath feel a hundred years old to be called Skip, the traditional nickname for a team's manager in baseball. Wasn't he just the hotshot rookie a blink of an eye ago?

Having Amber mistake him for someone like Diego ticked him off, even though the guy was nice enough. Estes had a world of problems of his own, and Heath was damn grateful to have escaped the worst of the groupie phase of his career unscathed.

"Yeah." Heath dropped onto a couch across from the TV, knowing he wouldn't be able to sleep for a while. "I just ran into a woman who thought I was you. Must be she knew you were staying here last week and somehow she got us confused. Too bad, because she seemed…"

He didn't finish the thought, knowing he shouldn't have this conversation with one of his players anyhow. Besides, how would he go about describing Amber? *Nice* didn't seem to cover it when she was sexy and straight-talking—or so he thought—and unexpectedly vulnerable.

"Was she hot?" In the background, Estes seemed to be waving off people who wanted to talk to him, their conversation interrupted by a muted "Not now." Then his attention seemed to return and he picked up where he left off. "You deserve someone totally hot, but someone with a good heart, too, Skip."

At twenty-three, Diego was older than a lot of rookies since they'd scouted him in the Caribbean where up-and-comers weren't involved in the baseball draft. Still, in the ways of the world, twenty-three was damn young, and in spite of the wise-sounding words Estes offered now, Heath knew the player had run aground in his own relationships.

"You think I'm taking dating advice from you, Estes?" Locker room gossip had it that Diego had been trying to get in touch with an ex-girlfriend back home in the Dominican Republic who'd dumped him before he came to the States a year and a half ago. Of course, there was a good chance she wouldn't want anything to do with a guy who had a huge female following and was frequently referred to as a ladies' man in the tabloids.

"Think what you want, but I know you shouldn't turn your back on the people who make you feel happy to be with them. That's too rare to give up for the insincere, fly-by-night types that surround us in this game."

Heath closed his eyes and pressed against the lids with his hands. His head hurt. And despite the anger he'd felt at Amber when he'd stomped out of her beach house full of righteous indignation, he felt regret flame to life.

"You there, Skip?" Estes prodded.

"I'm trying to decide if I'm just tired or if you're actually making sense." He was only giving the kid a hard time, since Heath hadn't been half as wise when he'd been twenty-three. Hell, he hadn't been half that smart when he'd gotten married and proved to be a supremely lousy husband.

The bark of laughter on the other end of the phone hinted at a dark bitterness.

"I had my heart gouged out with a spoon because I was too blind to recognize something good when I had it. Trust me when I tell you that I'm making sense." Estes muttered something about double-checking his car for his iPod and then he was gone—leaving Heath wondering what was going on between Diego and that ex-girlfriend of his to have the guy so turned around lately.

Diego's batting average had taken a nosedive in the last four games and Heath had hoped that the rest over the All-Star break combined with time at Heath's Nantucket place would straighten Estes out. But clearly, the player was still struggling with personal stuff.

Sad to think the twenty-three-year-old was giving *him* advice when it should be Heath helping his players wade through the challenges of playing in the big leagues. Was Estes right about not being so hard on people that made you happy? Heath flipped the channels on the television, thinking about how Amber hadn't really pursued him. Sure, she'd run into him at first, but then she'd disappeared into the crowd and had sought out privacy at a picnic table back at The Lighthouse. It wasn't as if she'd actively tried to hit on him.

He'd bought her the beer and invited himself to have a seat with her because she'd seemed down-to-earth. And yeah, maybe he'd kind of liked that she'd been totally unimpressed with him. So could he blame her now for not making a big deal about knowing his affiliation to baseball?

Thunking his head on the arm of the overstuffed sofa, he had the sinking sensation he'd been an ass to walk out on her earlier. He'd apologize tomorrow. Make it up to her somehow.

Because despite the fact that his career dreams were teetering on destruction as Estes's bat cooled off and the numbers in the loss column got higher, Heath had enjoyed himself tonight.

And that was the first time he could say that about any moment spent off the baseball field in a long, long time.

OF ALL THE NERVE.

Amber had repeated the phrase like a mantra to herself a few dozen times since Mr. Full of Himself had departed the night before. Now, she muttered it in between writing lines for the lone book review she'd promised to her editor during her vacation. A week off wasn't really a week off in her department these days.

She'd taken her laptop onto the patio of Rochelle's house, refusing to allow her conceited neighbor to think she was hiding from him after he'd walked out on her before the sheets were cold. Of course, the day's favorite phrase—*of all the nerve*—had the tendency to show up in her book review, insinuating itself into the text so that she had to keep going back and erasing it.

Honestly, where did the man get his arrogance? She'd refrained from calling Rochelle, preferring not to share the embarrassing details of her encounter with Heath. But part of her wanted to know more about him, if only to understand why he'd treated her the way he did.

He'd been kick-butt awesome one minute, making it his mission to prove to her she was a desirable woman worthy of sexual fulfillment. And when she remembered *that* Heath, she wanted to knock on his door and kiss him all over. But how could that same man turn so wretched the next moment, implying that she'd gone out hunting for a famous face?

"Amber?"

The sexy timbre of the familiar male voice rolled over her senses, making her aware of the new arrival on the other side of the patio railing.

She hadn't noticed his approach, but Heath stood there dripping wet from a morning swim, the rivulets of water running down washboard abs into soaking swim shorts.

"Amber?" she parroted, forcing her gaze back down to her computer's screen. "Are you sure you know who I am? I could be hiding the fact that I'm a nuclear physicist or a genetics engineer. Oh, wait, those aren't superstars in your book. I'd only have to be subversive about my identity if I was a rock star or an athlete, right?"

She typed another line of her book review and ended up with *of all the nerve* in capital letters.

"I came to apologize if I was out of line last night."

He leaned wet arms on the porch railing, putting his gorgeous, half-naked body far too close to hers.

"If?" She hit the delete key with too much force, pounding it over and over.

Too bad her life didn't come with a delete key. She'd have been tapping away at that sucker for months.

"I got to thinking about it last night after I got home and I realized I might have jumped to conclusions about your motivations."

Slamming her laptop closed, she gave him her full attention.

"You know, I purposely avoided you out here yesterday, not wanting to tangle with a man too far out of my league." The thought of it made her mad now. "As if your ability to hit a ball—or, I guess, tell someone *else* how to hit a ball—makes you any better than me. But I figured plenty of women come on to guys in your field so there was no sense in adding to your prodigious list of fans."

She stood, too irritated and—yes—hurt to have this conversation sitting still. Of course, hadn't she wanted to take a risk this week? To do something wild without considering every possible consequence?

She had to admit that Heath had helped her do just that. And he'd given her tremendous pleasure. Sure, the aftermath had stung. But at least she hadn't fallen for him first.

"You never mentioned that you knew who I was when I introduced myself." He seemed to have expected full disclosure on her part even though he'd waltzed into the bar last night throwing around an alias.

Didn't that seem just a touch hypocritical?

"It didn't occur to me you needed adulation for prancing around the baseball diamond in tight pants or sitting in a dugout spitting a wad of chew."

"I did already apologize," he reminded her, his jaw jutting forward with a stubborn tilt. "But I've been maneuvered and manipulated by groupies enough times that by now I—"

"You think I'm a *groupie?*" Any fear she had about growing tender feelings for this man vanished. She was so incensed she could hardly see straight.

"To be fair, you thought I was a Casanova young stud of a player." He stood toe to toe with her despite the railing in between them. "Maybe you thought I'd be an easy candidate for your full-court mating press."

His voice whispered along her senses despite the sting of the accusation. Incredibly, her body responded to his nearness, remembering all the ways he'd touched her the night before. All the ways he'd reassured her she was special. Worthy of his sole focus and attention to bring her to a place of total bliss.

"Looks like we both made some false assumptions." Her voice floated along on a breathless note, her skin tingling in spite of her brain's warning to bail.

"So why don't you let me make it up to you?" He edged his way around the railing to stand on the patio beside her. "I go back to work tonight now that my two-day suspension is over. We've got a home game against

Chicago. Why don't you make use of my ticket allowance and see the game from behind home plate?"

She felt her jaw slide open, surprised at the offer.

"I don't know anything about baseball." Did he want to see her again? Or was he just trying to smooth over the fact that he'd sprinted from her bed?

"Obviously." He picked up the tail end of her braid and used the tip like a paintbrush to trail lightly over her shoulder. "Anyone who can't tell a manager from a player is clearly not a fan. But have you ever been to a game?"

Heath studied Amber's dark eyes, hoping for a clue about what was going on in her head. He wasn't sure why he'd invited her, knowing he couldn't afford distractions this season. But he'd been wrong to jump to conclusions about her and he honestly wanted to end this on a good note.

No matter that he wasn't in the market for a relationship, Amber Nichols was the most interesting woman to cross his path in a hell of long time. She deserved better than his disappearing act.

Especially given what he knew about her past—that some guy had tried to pass off his own shortcomings as hers. The notion still pissed him off.

"No. I've never set foot in a baseball stadium."

A fact that further demolished his theory that she was a groupie.

"So don't knock it until you've tried it."

She hugged her laptop to her chest, planting a bulky physical barrier between them.

"I don't know." Frowning, she turned to look out toward the water where a young couple played in the surf with a loping St. Bernard. "Wouldn't a groupie try to wrangle good seats out of you?"

"A good groupie would be too busy throwing herself at me to worry about tickets."

The tide crashed higher on the shore beside them, spraying a fine mist along her skin. She rolled her eyes, but couldn't stifle a grin.

"As enticing as it sounds, I'm afraid I'll have to pass. Rochelle was kind enough to share the beach house with me this week so I could stock up on R & R and I plan to do just that." She nodded toward a picnic basket teetering on the end of the patio table, a blanket and a bottle of wine poking out one side.

"What's more relaxing than a baseball game?" He couldn't imagine anybody turning down seats at one of the most fabled stadiums in the majors—except for a New York fan, maybe.

She bit her lip, and he felt a phantom brush of her teeth along his skin, half remembered from the night before. The sight sent a surge of longing through him.

"Come on," he urged, knowing now he'd been dead wrong about her only being interested in him for his money or his fame. He'd had to talk her into sleeping with him, for one thing. Now he had to talk her into a date. "Give me the chance to make it up to you for thinking you were a groupie."

Finally, she nodded.

"Okay," she agreed, though she sounded as wary as if he'd just invited her skydiving. "But I'm not sure how I can make it up to you for thinking you were a home-run-hitting superstar. Seems to me I was having more kind opinions of you than you were of me anyhow."

He knew she was teasing. She wouldn't have any idea how tough it had been to leave his playing days behind and become a manager. Baseball had been the only thing that got him through the years after his mom died. The only thing that connected him to his father—a one-time pitcher for a west coast team who'd never married Heath's mother even after two kids together. Taking off the Aces' uniform after they'd had his last game had been a pain that didn't stop until he'd been hired back to manage the team. He'd only resigned himself to the gig since he was back in Boston blue and red.

Now he just needed to ensure this team played well enough to renew his contract. And with the pressure mounting from the higher-ups to turn the season around, that was going to be damn difficult.

"I'll figure out a way for you to make it up to me," he assured her, hiding how much the sport meant to him by distracting her with a quick kiss. Right over that plump lower lip that had taken his eye. "Game time is 7:00 p.m. and the tickets are at the Will Call window. If you stick around afterward, I'll give you the grand tour."

She looked dazed from the kiss, a thought that went a long way toward improving his mood. He didn't have any idea what he was doing by inviting her deeper into his world. All he knew was that after last night and the way she'd gotten under his skin, he wasn't ready to walk away yet.

5

"BUT I WAS SUPPOSED to walk away," Amber explained to Rochelle that night during the seventh-inning stretch at the Boston Aces' home game against the Chicago Flames.

Amber had coerced her friend into meeting at the stadium since Heath had left two tickets. Plus, Amber needed a cool-headed perspective on whatever was happening between her and the hot manager of the Boston team. Now, the former college roommates shared beers and a bag of peanuts after the Aces fell behind by a run. All around them, the crowd was on their feet singing about rooting for the home team. The night would have been really fun if she hadn't been a paranoid wreck about getting in over her head with a man who at this point was probably just being nice to her.

"I don't get it." Rochelle shook her head, long blond curls hopping around the shoulders of her shiny satin baseball jacket embroidered with the Aces logo from the seventies. "Why were you supposed to walk away? Who would ever suggest you ditch a hot guy like Heath?"

"Didn't I tell you about my plan for this week?" Amber hated throwing the peanut shells on the stadium floor, even though the rest of the fans seemed to. Instead, she balanced the box that had been their drink carrier on her lap and cracked them over the cardboard.

"I thought you wanted to meet someone." Rochelle cheered as the Aces came to bat and Diego Estes, the third baseman, warmed up his swing. She pointed to his photo as it flashed on the jumbo screen. "That's the guy who was staying at Heath's place when we were there last week."

Amber had to admit she never would have confused the young Latino with Heath if she kept track of the team at all. It was obvious the women went wild for Estes since the cheers took on a distinctly feminine sound.

"I did want to meet someone," Amber clarified, not wanting to talk about her mix-up the day before. "I also hoped to keep it uncomplicated and temporary. I don't need to romanticize every guy I get involved with, right?"

"You purposely sought out a one-night stand?" Rochelle's beer sloshed over the rim of the bottle as she whipped around to confront Amber.

"Well…" Hello, Awkwardness. "You encouraged me to have a wild affair, didn't you? I figured as long as the guy seemed game for a no-strings night, it wasn't a big deal."

Rochelle's eyes went as wide as her gold hoop earrings.

"You threw away your every cautious, careful instinct to have an affair just because that bozo Brent broke your heart?"

Amber appreciated her friend's concern—and her indignation on Amber's behalf. But she wasn't interested in bashing Brent so much as she wanted to move on. That meant figuring out what to do about Heath.

Shrugging, Amber washed down the last peanut just as the crack of a bat told her Diego had a hit. All around her, fans jumped to their feet and followed the progress of the ball toward the left field wall.

When the left fielder made a diving catch into that same wall, the fans fell back into their seats in unison with a communal wail of despair. As the next hitter came to the plate, Amber wondered how Heath was taking the catch in the dugout below. For now, however, she wanted to squeeze whatever wisdom she could from Rochelle about handling her upcoming sort-of date with Heath.

"I just want to see what it feels like to go out with someone without visions of happily-ever-after mucking it up for me. I've spent all my dating years either seriously involved or seriously single. I've never dated for fun."

"And you picked Heath Donovan for your 'fun' guy?" Rochelle toasted Amber with her beer. "He's hot, but he's also one of the most focused and intense coaches in the majors. Before that, he was one of the most focused and determined players. He's got a rep for being no-nonsense, even though my personal opinion is that he goes too easy on his veteran players."

The batter at the plate struck out, apparently, and the crowd erupted in booing at the umpire's call. Amber was more interested in what Rochelle had said about Heath being intense. It definitely might have been easier to keep things casual with a younger player—like she'd thought he'd been—but she wouldn't trade her night with Heath for one with another guy for anything in the world. She'd never felt anything close to the way he'd made her feel.

"Uh-oh." Rochelle clutched Amber's arm and pointed toward the home plate where Heath had made an appearance to speak to the umpire. "Heath got tossed from a game on the road three nights ago because he argued a strike three call too heatedly."

Amber watched him, the view from the front-row seats allowing her to see how good Heath looked in uniform. He wore a different jersey than his players—his shirt a navy V-neck with the team logo on one side as opposed to the buttoned vest over short sleeves that the team wore. But the gray baseball pants were just the same and—my—he sure wore them well.

"I've never dated a guy like that," Amber observed, as much to herself as to Rochelle. She really had no idea how to proceed.

No clue how to date just for fun, especially with a guy who was a no-B.S. straight shooter. He didn't seem to raise his voice with the ump, but he definitely got in the guy's face. Still, after he spoke his peace, he stalked back to the dugout without escalating the argument.

"Well, from where I'm sitting, he doesn't seem like the kind of guy who could do anything casually." Rochelle pulled out her phone to check an incoming text, probably an SOS from her husband who was home alone with their two small children. She popped the phone back in her bag and returned her attention to the game. "But maybe he'd be good for you since he's nothing like the guys you normally date."

"Nerdy professors?" Amber knew that was how Rochelle saw her taste in men. And Brent had taught a groundbreaking new style of psychotherapy at Yale.

"Cerebral types who spend too much time in their heads to know how to relate to people." Her friend zipped up her jacket and pulled her purse onto her shoulder. "I need to dash, Amber, but I think you'd be crazy not to at least see where this leads. Sometimes there's no predicting the people we're compatible with."

Or the people we lust after.

Amber couldn't help but acknowledge that with Heath, physical attraction came into play to a degree she wasn't used to. But she had no reason to think he was ready for anything more than a good time.

Amber kissed her friend's cheek and gave her a hug. "Thank you for coming and be careful heading home, okay?"

"You, too." Rochelle winked as she stood to leave. "But maybe you won't be heading home at all after the grand tour. Call me tomorrow, okay?"

Nodding, Amber waved goodbye and returned her attention to the eighth inning where the Aces' pitcher threw one strike after another to speed the game along. Nervousness set in about the night.

About Heath.

She had no idea what she was in for by spending more time with him. But as long as she kept her B.S. meter finely tuned and her heart out of the equation, she could afford to have a little fun. Couldn't she?

Getting into the spirit of the game as the Aces turned a double play, Amber congratulated herself on taking a risk. That had been one of her goals in this week all along. Now, the trick was not to get hurt.

"Did your two-game suspension help you cool off, Donovan?" some snot-nosed young reporter asked Heath at the postgame press conference.

Heath had been fielding questions about his blow-up on the strike call throughout the conference, amazed at how many ways sports journalists could ask the same damn thing. He yanked his gaze off the young reporter who—honest to God—appeared to be texting his story notes into a phone the size of a postage stamp. Collecting his thoughts, Heath stared at the door at the back of the room while trying to formulate a spin-proof answer that communicated exactly nothing.

And who should walk through the rear exit but a slender brunette with a long braid snaking over one shoulder of a white blouse. A green and pink paisley skirt fit her narrow hips perfectly, calling attention to long, tanned legs.

He'd seen her in the stands during the game, but those brief glimpses hadn't been nearly enough to satisfy the hunger for her that had developed. He'd planned to meet her near the Aces' front office after the interview, but he'd forgotten that she would have media credentials as a book reviewer for Boston's biggest paper. She wouldn't have been admitted to the brief press meet and greet otherwise.

"I wouldn't say I cooled off during the two-game suspension," Heath answered finally, knowing his response wasn't watered down enough. But he had a tough time playing it safe when Amber was around. "I've always approached the game with fire and intensity, and that's what I bring to the dugout as a manager. I'm not going to apologize for how I run the team."

Amber's gaze met his over the heads of forty other journalists, her dark eyes registering an elemental response when he talked about fire and intensity. Even across a crowded room, he felt the connection to her, a connection that went beyond the physical and appealed to him on every level. He remembered how offended she'd been at the suggestion of being a groupie, her huffy denial as she'd banged the keys on her laptop.

"I'm afraid we've run out of time," Heath began his standard routine for retreat, ready to exit and see where tonight led with Amber. Had she come simply to smooth things over and part on good terms? Or was she feeling the same call to explore their attraction?

"But, Donovan," the young reporter with the cell phone piped up again, pressing forward in the crowd so that he was tougher to ignore, "with less than a full season remaining on your contract, are you at all concerned about what the message from the Aces' administration is when they told you not to come to the ballpark for the two games during the suspension?"

After almost twenty years in the majors in one capacity or another, Heath knew he ought to remember that sometimes a ball came in from left field when you were least expecting it. He'd thought he was sailing into home and *Bam!* He was dead at the plate thanks to a hell of an arm on this kid.

The room went silent. Even though every person present knew the kid was out of line, every last one of them couldn't wait to hear Heath's answer. Except for Amber, every damn one of the people in this room knew baseball was Heath's whole life. He'd never hid that fact.

"I want what the administration wants—to win games." Heath congratulated himself on the perfect blandness of the answer even though the kid had tapped into his biggest fear with a sledgehammer. "We will continue to work toward that shared goal."

Switching off the microphone, Heath stalked away from the platform as the room erupted in follow-up questions. Fortunately, a throng of shouted inquiries were easier to ignore than single, well-pointed questions in a quiet crowd.

Still, he had to walk through the reporters to get to

Amber, and that made things a little stickier. By the time he reached her, she had the rear exit open and a paper plate full of pilfered munchies from the reception table in hand.

"Tough day at the office?" she whispered, offering him his choice of popcorn and peanuts.

"Damn vultures," he grumbled, keeping his head down to avoid any candid shots on his way out of the press room. "They circle and circle when they sniff out the least chance for blood." He took two cream puffs and steered her toward a bank of elevators, where he selected the last car. There, he inserted a key card to open the door.

"They are under a lot of pressure to produce stories that sell," Amber observed, taking in the Aces memorabilia on the walls all around them. "Their jobs depend on it."

He tugged her into the elevator cabin with him as a couple of reporters emerged from the press room.

"Don't tell me you're taking their side." He used his key card again inside to access their well-secured destination. "The media sharks are my mortal enemies."

"I thought that distinction was reserved for the New York Scrapers." She popped one last peanut in her mouth before taking a swig of cola and tossing the can.

"They're my enemy on the field. Off the field, it's the press." Heath couldn't avert his gaze from the glistening moisture on her lips. His finger gravitated to her mouth.

The softness of her beckoned, urging him to touch

and taste, to linger and savor. But the doors slid open to reveal their destination, distracting them both.

"Oh!" Amber's eyes widened at the sight in front of them.

The owner's sky box was perched high in the Aces' state-of-the-art stadium, a sleek retreat with all the comforts of a five-star hotel room except that on one side, instead of a wall, there was floor-to-ceiling glass overlooking the field. Wide-screen televisions filled another wall, providing the room's occupants with additional views of the games in progress. But the most breathtaking feature was the live view from the best seats in the house.

"Come closer." He urged her forward, tugging her into the plush box situated to the right of home plate, just three stories up. "This is something to see."

"It's okay for us to be here?" She looked around as if fearing they'd be caught on security cameras or something.

"It's the team owner's box. He keeps it for his family and friends, but every now and then he gives me the green light to use it." Heath had gotten the idea of doling out his Nantucket beach house to players from seeing the way the team's owner—Bob Tarcher—shared the box with people he wanted to encourage or reward.

"Really?" She sounded surprised as she stepped deeper into the room, and approached the bank of glass. "Those reporters made it sound like the team wasn't very happy with you."

"Tarcher is in my court, but there are more opinions

than his weighing in on whether or not I'll get to keep the managing job." He studied her face as she took in the view. "It's tough to coach in a city where you played, especially since I was a very visible, outspoken player."

"The prophet can't preach in his hometown?"

Not quite the metaphor he would have chosen. "I guess the locals know me a little too well. Or think they know me. I'm still paying for mistakes I made as a rookie player."

"The past definitely has a way of sticking with you," she mused, folding her arms as she tilted one shoulder into the glass wall and peered down.

"Speaking from experience?" He would be all too glad to deflect the talk from his precariously balanced career that could implode at any moment.

Besides, he realized he genuinely wanted to know more about her. He'd been so caught up in wanting her the night before that he hadn't really spent time delving deeper.

"Sort of." She pushed away from the glass to walk the perimeter of the room, her fingers gliding over the backs of plush gray couches. "I'm definitely pigeonholed in my job as the relentless fact-checker and hard-core book investigator."

"I thought you were a reviewer?" He watched as she admired the hardware on the kitchen cabinets.

"Me, too. But I uncovered a few holes in a celebrated writer's so-called autobiography and ever since my paper expects the same performance with every project I'm given. Authors hate it when they hear I'm reading their novel because they assume I'll be tearing it apart. And the sad thing is, I love books."

She rested a hip against the countertop and he couldn't help but remember what those same curves had felt like pressed against him.

"Are you under a lot of pressure at your job? Like the sports journalists?"

"I'm under a lot more pressure, actually. All the newspaper departments are struggling, but our readers love sports, so that section will always be a part of the paper. The books section isn't as much of a staple. So my job is a whole lot more dispensable." With one fingertip, she drew designs on the polished granite beside her. "In fact, half my department was cut six months ago. That's why I really needed the R & R this week. I've been doing the job of more than one person."

"It's impossible to keep up that kind of pace." He understood completely. "I tell my players that all the time. I send them to the beach house in Nantucket for the same reason you went. It's good to get away from everything."

He thought about her soaking up the sunshine on the patio the day before, slowly tanning those endlessly long legs. And it made him damn glad it had been him staying next door instead of any of his players.

"Maybe that's why your team wouldn't let you come to the ballpark for a couple of days," she suggested. "You needed to get away from it all, too."

He inched closer, needing to touch her.

"Well, if that's the case, it didn't work because I got

too damn distracted along the way." Nearing her, he slowed his step, waiting to see how she responded.

"Too many groupies mobbing you wherever you go?" She arched an eyebrow, but there was no fire behind the question.

"No. Just one really interesting woman." He reached to stroke a finger along her chin, tilting her face to his. "But I'm thinking maybe we could take a little of that R & R together."

"I don't find you very relaxing," she admitted, though she didn't move away from his touch. "Exciting, maybe."

"I'd settle for being a welcome distraction." He threaded his fingers through the hair above her loose braid at the back of her neck.

He could feel the rapid beat of her heart there, and he liked knowing that she wanted him. She presented such a cool facade to the world, he might not have guessed that she responded to him this way without those cues.

"I'm not ready for anything serious." She blinked up at him with worried eyes, perhaps concerned that this would offend him. "I just want to be honest with you about that."

He sensed a wealth of nuance in her warning. A whole host of potential complications. But being with her had made him realize he needed a diversion this season more than ever. Amber Nichols could be the antidote to the intensity that had gotten him in hot water with the team before. She'd talk to him about book reviews instead of baseball.

And when they weren't talking? Even better.

"Sounds like a deal to me." Tugging gently on her braid, he tipped her head back. He sealed his mouth to hers in silent promise.

6

HEATH HAD OFFERED to fly them back to Nantucket tonight since he had access to a plane and a pilot's license.

It was one of many moments in the evening when Amber had been reminded she was in over her head. Heath had apparently already retired from one extremely lucrative career and now begun another. The spoils of that career were evident in everything from that vintage bike he'd driven on Nantucket to the splashy SUV he retrieved in the parking garage underneath the stadium. Instead of the private flight, she'd agreed to a late dinner at his place on the mainland.

They drove there now, south of Boston toward Cape Cod where he had a house on the water.

"So you have a home on the Cape *and* on Nantucket?" She couldn't imagine the cost. The brownstone she'd bought in Boston proper had nearly broke the bank, but she'd been so determined to own her own place, she'd managed. Then the economy tanked and she'd had to rent out half of it to keep up the mortgage payments. "You must really love the northeast. If I could afford two houses, I'd look at the Florida Keys or Costa Rica or something warmer."

He shifted gears as they exited the main road winding along the coast. Here, the scenery changed from T-shirt shops and big, family-style restaurants to more residential homes dotted with the occasional church or post office. An old-fashioned ice cream parlor was one of the few signs that resort towns lurked nearby. Cars still filled the big parking lot, and vacationers crowded around picnic tables even though it was shortly before midnight.

"Actually, the place on Nantucket has been in my family for a long time. It's a great spot because property is tough to come by on the island, but it's rare I make it out there. I'm usually at my apartment in Boston or the house on the Cape since they're both closer to the stadium."

"You had an apartment in town and yet you opted to drive all the way down here tonight?" She craned her neck to see the rest of a seaside mansion surrounded by trees.

There were no streetlamps now, only the occasional landscape lights around the looming homes.

"You'll like the house better." He pulled into a driveway and rolled down his window to punch in a security code for a tall, wrought-iron gate. "The condo is just a place to crash when I'm too tired to drive home."

As the gate slid open, Heath drove around a paved

horseshoe to land in front of a sprawling white clap-board home perched on a bluff. On the side facing the driveway, two stories and a gabled roof presented a cozy exterior. But on either side of the home, stone steps led down to the shore side of the home, hinting at another level built into the hill. Already, Amber could hear the steady roll of waves off the Atlantic.

"Wow." She'd been to splashy publishing parties at places like this, but never as a private guest. "This is beautiful."

Not waiting for Heath to open the door, she let herself out of the SUV, ready to stretch her legs and get a closer peek at the house.

"Thanks." He joined her on the cobblestone path that snaked around the exterior, one hand landing in the middle of her back. "You want to check out the view?"

He led her toward the stone steps she spied, and she wondered if the home was so illuminated even when he was staying on Nantucket or traveling with the team. Lights dotted the flower beds of white hydrangeas and rhododendrons, making it easy to see her way down the wide, curving stairs to—

"Oh!" She gasped in delight as they reached the back courtyard where a table had been set outside on the cobblestones. Hurricane lamps sat on the table next to covered silver serving dishes. A filmy white canopy draped over a huge pergola, and purple lights filtered through the gossamer curtains, creating a magical set-ting for their dinner. Silver urns of fat white hydrangeas, alternating with large hurricane lamps, ringed the front of the bamboo table.

"I called a local caterer ahead of time," Heath explained, taking her hand and leading her to a seat. "I figured I owed you a nice dinner after I downed all the wings and ribs by myself last night."

In moments, he had the serving covers off the dishes and her plate filled with fresh seafood. Scallops and mussels, clams and a lobster tail competed for space alongside warm polenta and fat slices of tomato.

"IT WAS DELICIOUS." Amber wrapped her fingers around the stem of her wineglass and tipped the dry pinot grigio to her lips.

She didn't mean just the food. The whole night had been perfect, from the scenic drive to the gorgeous house, to the ocean view. And while she appreciated every moment of an enchanted evening offered by a man who appealed to her senses even more than the opulent lifestyle, Amber couldn't imagine how she could keep things uncomplicated with this kind of treatment. Every facet of the night had been romantic. Sensual. The ocean air caressed her skin with teasing breezes while the wine hummed pleasantly through her veins. She would have to tread carefully.

"There's more where this came from." He shoved aside his plate to lean across the table, piercing her with a hot stare.

"I couldn't eat another bite," she protested, hating to waste so much as a single scallop.

"No. I mean, more of this." He gestured vaguely to everything around them. "More dinners. More skyboxes. More beautiful places."

Frowning, she set down the wine, needing to make sure she had a clear head for whatever he was suggesting.

"What do you mean?"

"Come on the road with me this week. We've got a series in L.A. starting the day after tomorrow and I'd like to have you with me."

CANDLELIGHT FLICKERED between them, the golden glow reflected in Amber's eyes as she struggled for words.

Clearly, he'd surprised the hell out of her. But what did it hurt to ask?

"Amber, I don't have a normal job. I'm all over the country most of the year. It's lonely. It's isolating. It'd be great to have some company for however long you're willing to travel."

"I have a job." She shook her head, leaning back from the table and out of the warm ring of candlelight. "I couldn't possibly tell my editor that I'm not coming in for another week after I've already taken a vacation."

"But your vacation isn't over yet, is it?" He could figure a way around her objections. After all, he'd courted some of the best new talent in the world, convincing talented players from all over to sign with the Aces instead of the other teams.

"No. But I only have three days left." She folded her arms, her white blouse a bright spot in the shadows.

"So come to L.A. for those three days and try out life on the road. I guarantee you the most relaxing, fun three days ever. But if you want to go back afterward, I'll be sure you're in town on time if I have to fly you myself."

"You have a team to coach. A position to protect. Won't it interfere with your work if I'm—"

Standing, he moved to her side of the table and drew her to her feet, needing to make his case with every weapon at his disposal. He slid his arms around her waist.

"I'm not connecting with some of the players on my team, and I'm beginning to think it's because I can only coach the way I played. Maybe I need to relax a little so they can, too. And bottom line, I can't relax thinking about winning most waking seconds." He palmed her back through the smooth cotton. "You have a way of making me think about other things."

She laid her hands on his shoulders, a light touch that reminded him he hadn't gotten to do half the things he wanted to with her last night.

"All I'm asking is for you to give it a try. And if you have as much fun as I think you might, well, we'll see where we stand after the three days are up."

"I could never stay longer than that with the demands of my job," she assured him, although he noticed she'd stepped closer and her hands had started to roam over his shoulders. His chest. "But if you can promise to have me back in time—"

He captured her words with a kiss, unable to hold back any longer. Besides, he wanted her to remember what he'd said, and this way, he'd punctuated the statement in a way she couldn't forget.

"I wanted to take you for a walk on the beach," he whispered between kisses, his fingers already untwining her braid. "Or for a swim."

He'd wanted their first real date to be unforgettable, so good that she couldn't ditch him at the end of her vacation. But he'd been patient for hours, inhaling the scent of her clean skin without touching her, listening to her hum with satisfaction while she ate. He couldn't wait to touch her another minute.

"I'd take this over the beach any day." She flexed her fingers against his chest, brushing her hand lower. Lower. "I was starting to think I only dreamed last night."

Drawing her backward, deeper into the courtyard toward the house, he fumbled in his pocket for the key, but found his caterer had left the doors unlocked.

"It was better than a dream." He turned away from her to flip on a light inside.

She closed the door behind them and stepped out of her shoes before she flung her arms around him.

"Last night was pretty amazing." She did some kind of dip and shimmy move with her hips that stroked him in all the right ways. By now, her hair had unraveled completely, the kinky waves spilling over both their shoulders.

"And that wasn't a fluke." He held her hand, stilling her long enough to ensure she got the message. "It's going to be like that every time between us."

She leaned into him.

"Prove it." Unmistakable challenge lit her eyes.

The fire inside him leaped higher. Hotter.

And Heath realized that in eight thousand square feet of house, there was no bedroom close enough.

With a growled oath, he backed her into the den off the kitchen. A sofa would have to suffice. Amber didn't seem to mind, her fingers raking off his shirt in record time. She rained kisses down his neck and over his shoulder, a soft shower of sweetness while her hands went to work on his belt.

Finally, they reached the couch and he lowered her onto the soft blue tapestry. The lights from the courtyard filtered in through the windows, allowing him to see how good she looked stretched out on his furniture. Her blouse had come partially unbuttoned, revealing a hint of a creamy lace cup hugging her breast. A gold necklace with three pearls slid into the vee of her cleavage. Her skirt hem dipped between her thighs, the line askew so that he could see more of one leg than the other.

"So beautiful." He dropped a kiss there, high on one thigh, just to make her think about it.

She shivered and made a sweet sound in the back of her throat, making him recalculate his whole approach. They had all night.

"Let me," she urged, reaching for the belt she hadn't finished removing.

Moving away so she couldn't complete the task, he unfastened the clasp himself.

"Close your eyes." He placed his palm over her eyelids. "Don't think. Just feel."

"I haven't had a thought in my head for hours," she assured him, her whole body wriggling and restless until he planted another kiss between her thighs.

A slow, thorough kiss.

Her breath caught. Held. Her legs tightened and braced against the couch. Then, within a few heartbeats, her limbs went limp and languid. He reached to unfasten the rest of the buttons on her blouse, easily popping open one after another while he inched higher up her body with his mouth.

He had just reached the hem of her skirt when the doorbell rang.

And rang.

Amber bolted upright, straightening clothes and tucking strands of hair.

"It's okay," he assured her, not in any mood to see who was on his front porch at one in the morning. "They'll go away when we don't answer."

Riiingg!

Whoever it was really laid on the bell, drawing out the chime for five times longer than normal.

"It sounds urgent." Amber skittered away from him on the sofa. "I don't mind waiting while you see who it is."

As if he was in any condition to deal with company now.

"Shit." He indulged in the curse, feeling certain the situation warranted that and more. "I'll get rid of them, I promise."

If he only had a few days with Amber, he planned to make the most of them.

Riing!

"That's fine. Just, maybe, hurry." Amber handed him the shirt she'd torn off him earlier.

Grumbling and complaining all the while, he dragged his feet to give himself time to cool down. Heath elbowed his way into his shirt as he opened the door.

His third baseman, the notorious Diego Estes, stood on his front step. A black Mercedes coupe with a wrinkled front fender hissed in the driveway behind him.

"Thank God you're home, Skip." Diego ran a hand through hair that looked as if it had already been well raked. "I need a place to crash. I'm wrecked in more ways than one."

"Is anyone hurt?" A million ugly scenarios raced through his head.

"No." Estes shook his head, eyes widening briefly at the suggestion. "Of course not. I just forgot you had that damn security gate and I clipped the front of the thing before I put it in Reverse and punched in the code you gave me. As long as I don't have whiplash, no one's hurt."

Curses rose to Heath's lips as he thought about all the reasons why he should boot Estes off his team for pulling this kind of crap the night before the most important road trip of the season. Still, Heath reined it in because Estes was a five-tool player with an on-base percentage no one could deny.

"I have company, but if you just find a room and lock yourself in, I guess you can—"

"Hel-*lo*." Diego's eyes—even while under the influence and bleary from the demons that drove him—lit up at the sight of Amber.

Heath didn't need to turn around to feel her presence in the foyer behind him.

Just like that, he didn't feel so charitable toward his superstar guest, five-tool player or not. With Diego attempting a ludicrous once-over of Heath's woman, it made it damn easy to slam the door in his face.

"Forget it, Estes," Heath shouted through the oak barrier. "The pool house has a futon. You can crash there or I'll be on the phone to the cops so fast you can kiss your season goodbye."

Turning back to Amber, he was all too ready to take up where they'd left off. But the worried expression on her face suggested it wouldn't be as easy as returning to the den. For one, her concern nipped at his conscience, which informed him he needed to address this situation better.

"Shit." Opening the front door again, he let the third baseman in and hoped he could restrain from kicking his ass long enough to show Amber he wasn't such a bad guy.

No doubt about it, he was in for a crappy night.

7

"YOU'RE FORTUNATE you didn't hurt anyone." Amber poured Diego a second cup of coffee the next morning, wondering how Heath coped with a team full of young guys with too much money, fame and opportunity to get into trouble. "Thank God the only thing damaged in all this is the car and Heath's gate."

After Heath had let Diego in last night, he'd admitted he had been drinking, but Amber didn't think he'd been over the legal limit. Still, riding around upset and nipping from a flask was idiotic and asking for trouble.

She'd retired early, finding a guest bedroom and giving Heath privacy to talk to his friend. Apparently, Diego had been in a tailspin after discovering his old girlfriend back in the Dominican Republic had given birth to his baby after their breakup. Amber hadn't figured out all the dynamics of that relationship, but she'd learned that much from Heath when he found her before dawn and carried her back to his bed. She'd been too tired to capitalize on his nearness, and they'd spend those few hours together sleeping.

Her wild affair wasn't exactly off to an auspicious start. But then, she still had the rest of her vacation and a trip to L.A. ahead.

Now, Diego hung his head over a heavy stoneware mug while he sat at the breakfast bar. His eyes were rimmed with red, and his thick, dark hair had seen better days. Even so, Diego Estes was a tremendously attractive sight. Not that she'd trade the raw sex appeal of Heath for an instant. But objectively speaking, she could see where Diego might earn a reputation as a ladies' man. She'd bet it hadn't required much effort on his part to gather flocks of female followers.

"Did Heath tell you what happened?" He didn't bother stirring in any sugar, but he clanged a spoon around the mug anyhow, clearly tired and out of sorts.

"He said you were upset because you found out that you missed the birth of your son." She found herself identifying with the jilted girlfriend back in his home-town and strove not to sound judgmental.

Amber's mother had been two-timed by her first husband for months. Amber hadn't even been more than eight or nine in the aftermath of that hellish time, but she recalled what it was like to see her mom's heart broken into a million little pieces.

"I didn't just miss his birth. I've missed—" He shook his head. "If I had known I was going to be a father, I would have been there," he vowed, pounding the counter with his fist. "My son is six weeks old, and I never even knew about him until I tried calling my ex-girlfriend and her mother picked up with a kid crying in the background. The mom told me about my son. Jasmine never even tried to let me know."

Amber slid the coffeepot back onto the hot plate, hoping Heath wouldn't mind that she'd made herself at home. Or at least started the java. His sleek granite and stainless steel kitchen wasn't exactly what she'd call homey. But Amber didn't have any way of getting home until Heath woke up. And Diego seemed as if he needed comfort. The guy sounded sincere. Hurt. She debated what to say as Heath entered the kitchen.

Hair slick from his shower and his jaw freshly shaven, he wore a suit without the jacket. Charcoal pants matched the coat he pitched onto a nearby chair. A blue silk tie had the Aces logo embroidered in the middle, accentuated by a silver tie clip.

Bearing little resemblance to the laid-back biker dude she'd met on Nantucket, Heath was all business today.

"Maybe Jasmine knew you would be there if she told you, and she didn't want you to walk away from baseball and resent her for it later." Heath skirted around the breakfast bar and came straight to her.

She caught a hint of spicy aftershave as he captured her waist and kissed her hard on the cheek.

Oh. Hormones flared to life. Thoughts of Diego's problems fled.

"Do you know that?" Diego was on his feet, apparently plenty interested in Heath's take on the situation. "Did you know about this kid when you recruited me?"

"Hell, no." Releasing her waist, Heath helped himself to coffee, not seeming to mind that she'd raided his cabinets to find the necessary items. "Just an educated guess. But I've been around athletes and their girlfriends long enough to have seen this happen before."

Amber would have never suspected that Heath spent his free time dealing with things like this and she wondered if other managers were a part of their players' lives this way. Or did he have a special relationship with Diego because he'd personally recruited him?

Slowly, Diego sank back into his chair. Amber collected the things she'd assembled to make eggs for the hungover Diego, but Heath shooed her away and passed his mug of coffee to her.

Nice. She smiled as she poured in the creamer, pleased to see her seriously rich new lover didn't need to have all his food catered.

"You have been in the game a long time, haven't you, Skip?" Diego used the nickname for a manager, she'd learned, though it sounded old-fashioned and quaint to Amber's ears. "And your dad played before you, right?"

Heath's father had been a ballplayer, too? Her mug hit the granite harder than she'd intended, sloshing a bit of coffee over the side as she contemplated what she was doing dating someone involved in a major league dynasty.

"Sorry," she murmured, hastily wiping up the excess with a napkin.

"Yes. My father pitched for the L.A. Stars." His words were clipped, but a hint of pride remained. "His jersey still hangs in the stadium. You'll see it tomorrow at the field."

"Really?" Amber wondered why Rochelle hadn't mentioned that. "Does that make you baseball royalty?"

She said it to tease him, but he didn't crack a smile as he broke the eggs over a frying pan.

"He didn't acknowledge me until after I was drafted. He never married my mom."

Heath tapped one shell after another until the pan was full, focusing all his attention on breakfast. But Amber had been forced to share the story of her own family history enough times to know you didn't spill those details without an answering spear of pain.

Diego seemed oblivious, though, still stirring black coffee. "Maybe your mom was like Jasmine. She wanted your dad to have his career."

"Could be," Heath agreed easily enough, retrieving plates from an overhead cabinet. "Families make sacrifices all the time to see their own go pro. You can fly Jasmine and your son up here to spend time with them, but don't blow it for them and mess up the career. You've got a hell of a lot to be proud of, and so do they."

Amber soaked in the import of that advice while Diego accepted a plate full of eggs.

The two men moved on to discussing their chance of a win in L.A. and Amber used the time to think about what Heath had said. Did he speak from experience and a real desire to reassure Diego? Or was Heath's main goal just to retain a successful player on his roster? He certainly had reason to want the team's best hitter focused on his game.

But she hated to think Heath would ever suggest one of his players ignore a son in favor of making a name for himself in the big leagues.

Not that she planned on getting caught up in Heath's life. She was just here for the road trip and the fun. Relaxation and romance.

Right?

"Amber?"

Heath's voice filtered through the worries chasing around her brain.

"Yes?" She realized she hadn't touched the plate he'd put in front of her.

"When you're ready, I'll run you back home so you can pick up some things for the trip." He studied her curiously over his coffee cup.

"That would be great." It would give her a last chance to back out if she discovered Heath was the kind of manager who told his players whatever they needed to hear in order to show up at the park every day.

And if not? If Heath really walked the walk of a child left behind by a father too famous and important to be bothered by his own progeny? She would have far too much in common with her hot baseball manager lover.

She was screwed either way. So far, she was down in the count for keeping things light and uncomplicated.

HE'D BEEN AN IDIOT.

Diego dove into the pool behind his manager's house, taking advantage of the cold, clean water to clear out his head.

He hadn't just used poor judgment last night, when he'd been tipping a flask of Wild Turkey to drown the pain of discovering he had a son he'd never known about. That ranked high on the idiocy scale. Diego had been operating on diminished gray matter since he'd left Jasmine behind to pursue his career in the States. He'd been home once ten months ago, and there'd been that one time they'd caved to the heat that always flared between them. That must have been when she'd gotten pregnant.

He flipped underwater and pushed off the side of the pool, holding his breath while he swam the length of the in-ground monstrosity again.

He'd loved Jasmine. But they were young, and their dreams were so different. She wanted to work with kids who'd grown up in at-risk communities—the places where they'd come from. He couldn't wait to get out of there and live the good life. Why couldn't she understand that with the money he pulled down here, he could buy her a whole damn center to take care of those kids? He wished Jasmine understood there were different ways to help out—that he wasn't turning his back on the people at home. Sure, she was trying to show kids how to have a better life—but so was he.

His lungs burned as he started his third lap of the pool, his oxygen-starved blood making him light-headed. Enlightened. Because sure enough, he saw now he wasn't living the good life alone in the States, hounded by females who didn't care about him half as much as they cared about the houses, clothes and cars that his kind of income could buy.

He broke through the surface of the water, gasping and spluttering but never breaking pace as his arms pinwheeled around for one stroke after another. Jasmine had just been smarter than him. She hadn't dumped him a year ago because she was jealous of his soon-to-be fame or because she was trying to give him an ultima-tum about staying with her. She'd simply known what she wanted and known that she didn't need a fat bank account to be happy.

Or to make their kid happy.

Hell, maybe Jasmine had saved their son from being raised by a loser who still kept a flask of Wild Turkey around like some kind of high-school kid.

Screw. That.

Diego pushed himself deep under the water again, but this time he opened his eyes to see what was in front of him.

Baseball wouldn't be there for him if he kept up the hitting slump. But Jasmine and his kid—Alex, she'd named him—would be a part of him forever, no matter what.

He wasn't going to mess around with his life anymore, now that he knew what he had to do. He would call her tonight and ask for another chance.

"HOLY COW." Heath took two steps into Amber's Boston apartment and wondered what he was getting into. "Don't tell me you've read all these."

Books filled every conceivable inch of the space. Built-in shelves butted up against furniture racks so that the walls looked as if they were covered with spines for wallpaper. The whole place was bright, though. She must have covered her collection in paper jackets of her own making because all the spines were mostly white with brightly colored strips in the center where the title and author went. All the white books with red strips were grouped together. Then white with yellow. White with green. Between the books a few odds and ends were stashed to break up the marching rows—a striped hat box, a ceramic cow, a fat gold ship's bell.

"I've probably read about half from cover to cover. A quarter I've used for reference and the rest are all on a growing list of things I'd like to read."

Amber had already disappeared somewhere in the apartment, her voice raised enough for him to follow the direction of it. He wound around an old-fashioned tea cart to catch a glimpse of her in a room that looked like a bedroom with an office on one side. No, more like a library with a desk and a bed.

"I didn't fully appreciate what it meant to be a book reviewer." He ran a finger along a few of the titles, admiring the paper jackets, which were all pale yellow in this room. "Is there some significance to the color coding?"

"It's my nod to the Dewey Decimal System without having to broadcast the numbers." She pulled open a closet door and emerged with a suitcase. "I know the greens are bios. Yellow is history, and so on. But there aren't many books here that are related to my reviewing work. Sadly, this is the extent of my personal entertainment most days."

"Not this week, it's not." He'd been dying to get her alone ever since their date had been busted up by Diego's appearance the night before. He cornered her by the closet. "You've got me and you've got baseball to keep you entertained. Very much in that order."

He cupped her shoulders, slowing down her brisk movement around the room. Not until then—when it took her a long moment to say anything—did he realize she hadn't said much on the ride over here today.

"Can I ask you a question?" She didn't relax into his touch, putting him on guard.

"Have you changed your mind about this week?" He suddenly recognized that he wanted her to accompany him with a fierceness that surprised the hell out of him.

"No." The tension didn't leave her shoulders. "I just wondered about what you said to Diego at breakfast. That stuff about your dad."

In the same way one player's anxiety about a game could affect a whole locker room, Amber's tension was now his own. But he'd dodged this kind of thing from reporters for years. He had no intention of trotting out anything more than the status quo. His time with Amber was supposed to be about de-stressing, not confronting skeletons in the closet.

"Fire away." He forced his voice into that easy, trust-me octave that could convince the press—and his rivals—that a star player's injury was nothing serious.

Sometimes being a manager meant being a master of spin.

"Did you let Diego think you had something in common with him to make him feel better? Or do you honestly believe his playing career made it okay that you were ignored by your father?"

Heath blinked. Processing.

He was pretty sure his trust-me expression had frozen onto his features.

"Wow. I forgot what a straight shooter you are." He'd never met a woman like her. Direct. Forthcoming. No games.

Hell, he didn't know if he could match that uncompromising honesty. And he'd been worried about her playing him to get near a star? The idea had become so ludicrous to him in the past twenty-four hours that he wondered how he'd ever dreamed it up in the first place.

"I don't mean to pry." She backpedalled, no doubt sensing she'd stepped in over her head. "I was just blown away to think you could forgive a father for something like that, but then again I really hated to think you'd say that to Diego just to—"

"Don't even finish the thought." He lowered himself onto her bed beside the suitcase she'd placed there. "I would never concoct a story to manipulate my guys like that. I might hype up Boston to get them to play for me, and I might talk up east coast women like they're the hottest to ever walk the earth to tempt the holdouts. But I'd never be dishonest with them."

She moved toward a dresser tucked between two bookshelves and opened the drawers, top to bottom, pulling out shorts and tank tops. The sight cheered him, assuring him that he would have her all to himself tonight.

"I should have known." She tossed the assortment of cotton in the suitcase and stepped closer to him. "You were good to Diego last night, letting him have a place to stay. And you must have been trying to help him out last week by giving him some time at the Nantucket house."

"It's tough for the young guys. Everybody wants something from them. They don't know who to trust. Most of the people they meet only want access to a lifestyle. So they romanticize old relationships because at least before they made it big, they knew they were in-volved with people who genuinely cared about them."

"And you can relate because you've been there." Amber wrapped her hand around his.

He wanted to pull her into his lap and hold her there,

but he knew the moment called for some nod to her original question about his father.

"Relating to the players is a big part of the job. But I don't bring up the topic of my dad too often since I don't like being compared to him. I still don't see him all that much, but I forgave him a long time ago for ditching the parenting role. There are some people who do more damage than good by hanging around."

She frowned and he sensed that comment only stirred up more questions on her part. Damn it. Maybe they weren't going to be able to keep things simple between them, after all.

But then her expression cleared and she nodded thoughtfully.

"Okay. One last question before I finish packing." She pinned him with a level stare and he wondered what she could fire his way next. Something about his screwed-up childhood? His failing career?

He steeled himself.

"What I really want to know is—and be honest—do you think it makes me less of a nerd if I told you I read wearing—" she dug into a drawer and shook out a tiny scrap of lace and satin that blew his mind "—nothing but this?"

8

MAYBE AMBER HAD BEEN a coward to back down from the conversation that would have helped her understand Heath better.

But by the relief in his eyes when she'd let him off the hook made her feel as if she'd just given him a Christmas present. She enjoyed making him happy. She still couldn't believe she had that power over this sexy man.

He tugged her closer until she stood between his legs where he sat on her bed. His suntanned skin made him look like a swarthy, stubble-faced pirate on a sea of white chenille. He slipped the satin merry widow from her fingers and let it fall to the bed, all his focus on her.

"You'd be sexy wearing anything. And it's not the books that run the risk of making you nerdy." A grin teased his lips as he bracketed her waist in his hands. "It's the fact that you dressed them all up in matching outfits like paper dolls."

His fingers slid under her blouse to palm her bare spine. She liked fitting there, between his thighs, warm and safe and teasing. In fact, she liked everything about the man and the moment, including the knowledge that he seemed to want her as much as she really, really wanted him.

"I'll have you know that my volumes will last longer because of those book jackets." She steadied herself against him, bracing her hands on his shoulders as he tipped her forward, closer.

"Face it, Amber. Color coding your book covers is treading strongly into obsessive-compulsive terrain." His hands spanned her ribs and skimmed upward, higher, until he cupped her breasts in his palms.

Pleasurable shivers arced through her, heating her blood and reminding her what sex had been like with him the first time. How generous he'd been. How he'd made her feel special when she'd been flat-out afraid of failure.

"I'll stick with nerdy, thanks. And at least here we don't have third basemen ringing the doorbell to interrupt."

A fortunate thing, because she really wanted to see where this would lead. Her heart skipped and started a jerky rhythm as Heath eased the cups of her bra down. Capturing the taut peaks of her breasts between his fingers, he rolled the tips against his knuckles. His eyes never left her face, cataloging her expression and response.

Could he tell that he made her insides melt?

"You make a good point. Because if the phone rings or someone knocks on the door now, I'd really like to ignore them." He released her long enough to unhook the bra and tumble her down to the bed with him. Over him.

"Lucky for you, reviewing so many books every month seriously cuts into my social time. My friends don't ever come around to try to drag me out of the house anymore." She also didn't usually have a hot man in her bed that made her feel beautiful.

But this week was all about pushing out of her comfort zone.

"Lucky for you, I think book reviewers are really hot." He tugged her blouse off, whipping it across the room as if it had been a frustrating impediment to the breasts he now kissed and licked.

He didn't rush, even with a plane to catch in a couple of hours. Instead, he flipped her to her back and nudged her suitcase off the bed with his toes.

"It's a blast being lucky," she murmured, her eyelashes falling to half-mast with the instinct to shut out everything but what Heath made her feel. She couldn't close them completely, though, not with the temptation of peeking at Heath's hard, honed body.

What an incredible-looking man. She had never taken the time to salivate over athletes on television before. First, because she didn't really watch sports, or much TV for that matter. Second, because she'd unfairly stereotyped athletes as jocks who were more interested in bodies than brains.

And while that hadn't turned out to be true with Heath—clearly he appreciated her brain or he wouldn't have asked her to spend more time with him—she had to admit that she'd begun to see the appeal of raw male muscle.

It was so much more than the ability to swing a bat or run fast. It represented a dedication to excellence that she'd never thought about before. Plus, just the feel of that sinewy strength pressed against her body put her halfway to orgasmic.

Now, he unfastened her jeans and peered up at her with a dark, sexy stare that made her smolder.

"No more thinking," he reminded her, just the way he had the last time he sent her careening into sensual bliss.

For a woman who'd built a career on thought and words, she had to smile at the dictate. It warmed her heart that he would remember her hang-up and caution her to avoid it.

"My brain is blank." She closed her eyes now, settling the restless churn of thoughts so she could concentrate on just this moment.

He cradled her cheek and skimmed a thumb along her jaw.

"You can still look at me." His voice in her ear startled her eyes open as much as the words. "I like your eyes on me."

They connected in that moment. Amber felt the jolt as their gazes met. Locked. Whereas two nights ago had been all about want, need and desire, another element awakened just then to add to the mix of emotions.

Amber could not analyze it, though. Heath had succeeded in stripping her down to her panties, and he palmed the warmth between her legs through the white silk.

She gasped at the feel of him there, her mouth falling open while her pulse throbbed fast against his hand.

"That's better," he crooned, encouraging her with soft words as his fingers played over her sensitive flesh.

She clutched his shoulders, knowing if she could keep him there—right there—she would be spiraling off into bliss in no time.

HEATH LIKED THE BITE of Amber's short nails in his skin, the soft sting against his back telling him that she was long past thinking and ready to feel.

He'd remembered that part from the last time he'd been able to touch her. Take her. She'd been thoughtful and still for a while, and then something had hit a switch for her and she'd lost herself to the moment so fully that he'd hardly recognized his brainy, cerebral lover.

The nails in his shoulder told him she'd arrived at that place now, and he felt like a few million bucks to know he could do that for her. It made holding back so damn worthwhile. He'd been ready for her since the previous night, so ready that he would have gladly jumped her the second they'd walked through her apartment door. But he'd waited and—damn—payback was sweet.

The soft cries in his ear were like Morse code for

what she wanted, the notes higher and sweeter when she was getting close to the edge. He could have brought her there quickly, her body hot and wet and very ready for him.

But he drew out the pleasure to make it last for her. When she teetered too close to that sensual precipice, he allowed his fingers to wander away and tug her panties off. Or trace a damp pattern with her wetness along the inside of her thigh.

"Heath." She flexed her fingers against his shoulder, her thigh hitching higher along the outside of his leg. "I'm so close. So—"

A low moan trembled through her. Everything remained suspended for a long moment. Then her cry filled the room, drowning out the soft whir of a ceiling fan overhead.

He held her tighter, absorbing the shock waves that rocked her body inside and out, anchoring her through the pleasure. He wanted his scent on her body and his voice in her ear when she came. If he only had these days with her, he would imprint himself on her so thoroughly she would never forget.

When the tremors eased, he released her enough to retrieve a condom from the pocket of his jacket that he'd tossed on the pillow.

"I'll do it." Amber surprised him by snatching the wrapper from his hand. Then, she seemed to second-guess herself. "Can I?"

Rolling onto his back, he gave her room to work. Her cheeks were still flushed from the orgasm, her dark hair slipping free from the tight braid so that she looked like a sweet, sexy mess.

"I'm yours to do with as you see fit." His blood ran hot and his cock had been stiff for hours. "But you might want to be, uh, no-nonsense in your approach. I'm loaded and ready."

Her gaze flashed to his and he could see the nervous excitement there.

"I'll try not to get too distracted." She had the wrapper off and prophylactic in hand. Her gaze dipped southward toward his boxers, erected like a damn circus tent. "But it might not be easy."

She might as well have stroked him with her tongue. His cock stirred and throbbed. Seeming to sense the urgency, she worked to free him from the boxers. Still, by the time she rolled the condom on, he had no choice but to take charge again before he lost it all over her.

He thrust deep, burying himself inside her. Then stayed there for a long moment to collect himself. Sweat popped along his forehead and his back, the effort of holding back rapidly catching up to him. He bracketed her shoulders with his hands in the bedspread, levering himself above her to find the right angle that would take her to that sensual ledge all over again. This time, she seemed to know what she wanted, wrapping her legs around his hips and lifting to meet each thrust.

As he followed the song of her gasps and moans, he didn't let go until he heard that high, keening note in her throat. Only then did he move as deep, as hard and as fast as he wanted, chasing that perfect pleasure until it steamrolled him.

Bliss filled his veins like an illicit drug, a heady rush that bowled him over and made his blood boil. It was a union as un-freaking-real as anything he'd ever felt in his life.

He had no business getting involved. No right to bring a woman on the most important road trip of his life.

Furthermore, the brainy reviewer and the driven athlete made no sense together.

But no matter that nothing added up. He couldn't wait to have this woman all to himself.

9

AMBER HANDED HER champagne glass to the flight attendant on her way off the plane with regret, thinking she could get used to flying first-class.

Hitching her bag on her shoulder, she followed a few men in suits who'd sat in front of her on the commercial flight, winding through the jetway and into the concourse. Heath had apologized for not being able to seat her on the team's chartered aircraft, explaining that he could only bring the team, the trainers and Aces' staffers on board. But he'd meet her at LAX as soon as her plane landed since they got in at the same time.

No skin off her nose. She'd never experienced the luxury of a seat on an airline that left her room to cross her legs and served her peanuts before anyone else even got on board. She couldn't imagine what a first-class seat reserved just hours in advance must have cost. Probably enough to pay her mortgage for a month. Possibly two.

Her cell phone buzzed in the pocket of her long linen

shorts and she pulled it out to answer as she dodged two little boys chasing each other while engaged in a swordfight with paper straws.

"I'm never flying coach again," she answered, knowing Heath would be on the other end, looking for her.

She stood on her toes to try to see him ahead of her as she rode the escalator down to the exits for ground transportation.

"Amber?" The voice in her ear was not the low, sexy growl she thought it would be.

In fact, just then she spotted Heath waiting for her by the doors, just as he'd promised. And he didn't have a cell phone in his hand.

"Brent?" Her forward progress slowed. Halted.

A woman behind her bumped into her and then went around with a muttered oath about cell phones being the work of the devil.

"Where are you?" her ex-boyfriend asked, not bothering to answer her question.

And well, duh, she recognized his voice just from hearing him say her name. How many weeks had she gone hoping he'd give her a call and see the error of his ways, if only so she could tell him to taking a flying leap off a short building?

"I just touched down in L.A." She didn't tell him to make her life sound exciting—it hadn't been until two days ago—but so he wouldn't fret. One thing she'd credit Brent with was that even if he thought she was an Arctic breeze in the bedroom, he would still worry about her if she refused to tell him where she was. "I'm meeting some friends."

Up ahead, Heath appeared concerned. He started toward her as she ducked out of the rush of humanity toward the exits. Her butt hit the wall of free phones for local hotels.

"You're in Los Angeles?" He didn't sound relieved to know where she was. "Your paper is on hard times, your section might get scrapped, your job is in jeopardy and yet you found time to make a run for the Pacific? What the hell are you doing there?"

She straightened, not appreciating his tone one bit.

"I'm sure it's no concern of yours," she told him coolly, half wishing she'd told him she couldn't talk because she was in bed with her new lover. Her eyes went to Heath, who was only a few steps away now. "What did you want, Brent? I'm really busy."

"I'm sorry." His tone was conciliatory. "I e-mailed you a couple of days ago to see if you had time to talk. When I hadn't heard back—"

"You hoped to talk?" She wished that sentiment didn't make her feel like a wrung-out washcloth, but it did. "Doesn't that fall into the too-little-too-late category?"

She wanted to hang up on him. Truly, she did. Heath stood beside her with his overwhelming sexiness and his thoughtful concern for her, having paid a boatload to transport her here for a few days. But how could she cut Brent off at the knees when Heath would vacate her life and leave her with the Brents of the world?

As much as she resented Brent personally, she owed it to herself to try to recognize what went wrong with him. That way, she would do better the next time when she—inevitably—ended up with that same type of quiet, practical, steady guy.

"I just need to see you, okay? I need to explain about some of the things that happened. Will you call me when you get back in town?"

Her eyes slid to Heath, who tugged her rolling suitcase out of the path of pedestrians. He withdrew his cell and made a quick call of his own.

Damn it, she wouldn't waste Heath's time or hers talking to someone who'd already tossed her aside.

"I'll think about it. But I have to go now."

With a muttered goodbye, he was gone. Leaving Amber confused and a little off her game. She needed to relax. Play. Enjoy a man who only wanted a good time.

"Is everything okay?" Heath asked her, shoving his own phone back into his pocket. "I asked the cab to wait, but if you have things you need to take care of, I can let him go."

"No." Flustered, she gripped the handle of her suitcase and jammed her phone into an exterior pocket, not wanting to answer it again for a long time. "My flight was great and I'm ready to be with you."

Heath took her suitcase from her and nodded toward the double doors ahead to indicate they should get moving.

"Is that because you are totally enamored with me? Or because Brent was too little too late?"

"All of the above." She wasn't surprised he'd overheard. And she had nothing to hide.

"You want to talk about it?" He held the door for her even though he was the one with all the bags.

She had to admire the chivalry.

"There's not much to talk about. We dated for nine months and I thought we had carved out an intelligent, balanced relationship. He thought I had the emotional quotient of a computer. End of story."

She slid into the cab he indicated, waiting inside while he gave the bags to the driver. Palm trees and the pastel walls of a nearby parking tower told her they were in California. Otherwise, the airport hummed with the same kind of traffic as any other major hub. Hotel and rental car shuttles vied for the best position near the curb while airport security motioned cars and people to where they belonged.

Eighties tunes played on the cab's radio, but the young driver turned down the music when he got into the car. Heath directed him to a hotel and they were on their way, cocooned in semiprivacy with the plastic divider closed and cabbie singing along to The Bangles.

"I only picked up the phone, by the way, because I figured it would be you looking for me," she explained, feeling awkward about the whole business.

Brent had no right to butt into her life after he'd told her they needed time apart. No, after he'd dumped her.

"You don't believe in caller ID?" Heath asked, picking up her hand where it lay on the seat between them and folding it into his own.

She warmed to his touch. To him. How was it she found him so easy to talk to when she'd been reticent around guys her whole life? She made a mental note to try to find out if he had any secret nerdy tendencies—that might help explain her feeling more at home around him even though she didn't know about them.

"I was anxious to tell you how cool it was to fly first-class so I just answered the phone and blurted that out, thinking it had to be you on the other end."

He laughed as the cab pulled out of the final airport exit and out onto a highway that was massive even by Boston standards.

"I'm sorry that wasn't me on the phone. I would have liked to have had that conversation with you." His eyes told her that he would like a lot of other things with her, too.

A flutter started in her chest, her breath catching. How did he make her think about getting horizontal with him without even trying?

"I don't act like myself around you," she admitted, having lost most of the filters that usually helped her navigate conversation with men. "Usually I check caller ID. I check e-mail. I measure my words. I overthink things. With you I'm really shooting from the hip and I'm not sure why."

The cab wove through three lanes, dodging and darting around traffic so that she scooted closer to Heath. If they got into an accident, she'd prefer to have her body ejected near his.

"Vacation romance, maybe. That's why the kids have so much fun on spring break, I hear." He pointed out the Hollywood sign up on a hill.

"Maybe." She wasn't sure at all. "I would have never even considered a vacation fling until recently. Usually, my vacations in the past meant I read for pleasure instead of work."

"You're a real wild woman, Amber." He released her hand to tug on her braid.

"You see my point? I'm so totally not. I would have thought I'd be terrified to be with someone famous and accomplished—"

"Let me stop you right there." His hand fell to her thigh, and he nudged her whole body to face him. "I'm a divorced, washed-up player trying like hell to stay in the majors. There's a good chance they'll boot my butt out the door before the season even ends. I'm just trying to give it one last battle, all the while knowing I need to prepare myself somehow if it all falls apart."

Flashes of that intensity Rochelle had talked about glittered hard in his eyes. He really saw himself that way. *A washed-up player.*

"That's your secret nerdiness." She should have seen it all along.

"What?" He looked at her as if she'd sprouted an extra head.

"Sorry. I just had been thinking earlier that maybe I relate to you because you have some nerdiness of your own stashed away in that gorgeous exterior. You know how I'm a book dweeb with my matching dust jackets? Well, you're not exactly a devil-may-care, swing-for-the-fences kind of baseball player that saunters in for his five minutes of fame and retires on a fat salary to write a book. You're a baseball nerd. This sport means everything to you."

Heath told himself she was babbling. That her light-bulb moment in the back of the cab was cockamamy B.S. and the only reason they really related was hot sex.

But the longer the words rolled around in his head, the more he wondered if she had a point. Not that he could truly speak to the reason she liked him.

And she did—he could tell by the way she moved closer to him whenever he was near. The way her eyes would find him in a crowd with unerring speed, drawn to him as powerfully as his gaze was to her.

No, he wasn't sure what had made his brainy book reviewer notice him instead of some professor type who knew all about the ancient dance of gender politics and the assorted think-y stuff that interested her.

But he knew she had a point about his lifelong fascination with baseball. He'd never played the sport like a mere *game*. For him—corny as it sounded—baseball was poetry and a philosophy. An approach to life. It colored his perspective of everything from how he read the newspaper (box scores first) to how he interpreted the weather (rainy years in the Caribbean meant less

practice for future prospects and possibly a worse crop
of players).

Other guys played the game. They passed through the
sport year in and year out, going on to do other things
after they left the majors. Heath had adopted a way of
life where the world only gave you so many strikeouts.
A bad day at bat meant hours in the cage to straighten
out your swing.

That was why he couldn't mess up his last stand as a
manager. He had to stay in the sport because it was the
only place where life made sense to him. He understood
the rules. And somehow, being with Amber while he led
his shaky team through a key series felt like the right
thing to do. Before he'd met her, he'd gotten ejected
from a game because he'd been so damn tense, and that
wasn't serving the greater needs of an uneasy young
team that needed leadership. His veteran players were
letting him down in that department, so he probably
needed to step up and be more of a hard-ass with the
younger kids. Basically, he had to have his head together.
And Amber made him feel more level than he'd been in
a long time.

"I think we're here," she pointed out, nodding toward
the old-school Beverly Hills hotel that would house the
whole team for the next few days. "Sorry if I was out
of line about the baseball thing. I'm sure you couldn't
be nerdy if you tried."

She bit her lip and didn't try too hard to hide a smile.
Ragging on him again.

God, she was a handful. He couldn't imagine what

this wisecracking, honest, sexy woman had ever seen in the stodgy, idiotic Brent back home. She seemed to have opened her eyes, though. She was here with him in L.A. instead of listening to Mr. Intellectual catalog faults she didn't have.

If nothing else came of this road stand, Heath planned to make damn sure Amber Nichols knew her own worth. He was just the man to show her how irresistible she was.

10

"OH, MY GOD, that's Heath Donovan."

The same phrase, with minor adjustments, was whispered, squealed and hyperventilated throughout the upscale Beverly Hills hotel lobby. Amber must have heard it a dozen times already and they hadn't even hit the elevator bank yet.

She'd been so busy preparing herself for the new experience of vacationing with a hot guy just for fun—a wild and utterly new venture for her—that she hadn't thought to steel herself for the scores of female fans eyeing Heath.

As they wheeled bags toward the elevator banks, their room keys already in hand thanks to the advance legwork of the travel administrator, women of all ages paused to swoon. Amber knew they weren't just looking at Heath. Diego and the rest of the team caught a fair share of admiring stares. But Heath was still a star in his own right, his playing days not so far behind him that he didn't have a fan following in the lobby. One woman grabbed her girlfriend's arm and jumped up and down in high heels with the friend's shoulder for leverage, panting, "Heath, Heath, Heath, oh, my God, it's Heath," as they walked by. Amber tensed, debating ducking and running for cover, but Heath gave a terse nod and shouldered right through the crowd, letting one of the team's assistants deflect the attention.

When Amber and her famous companion entered the elevator, the doors closing them into semiprivacy with the catcher Brody Davis and pitching sensation Jay Cannon, she had to give herself a shake to call back reality.

"You guys have shown me what it means to be invisible," she announced to no one in particular, surprised not one of them mentioned the hubbub they'd caused. "You would think people in L.A., of all places, would be accustomed to seeing a few famous faces."

"My wife used to try to smuggle me through a back door when she traveled with me," the catcher admitted, grinning. "But somewhere along the line she decided she'd rather tattoo herself to my side and march me through the front to make sure the women of the world know I'm taken."

The gold band around his left ring finger glinted in the fluorescent light as he held the elevator door for someone hopping on the lift on the third floor.

"I don't even hear it," the pitcher joined in, pulling free the earbuds he wore, the sound of Metallica evident even four feet away from him. "My dad says to keep your head in the game, not in the fame."

He tucked the buds back in, and Heath nodded affirmation.

"Wise man."

He didn't say any more, however, leaving her in the dark about how he reacted to his apparent legions of admirers.

On the sixth floor, the players piled out with their bags. Heath reminded them to be at the ballpark early the next day and then hit the button to put them up one floor higher. Amber remained silent in the interim since a teenage boy rode with them. At their floor, she stepped into the hall and a new wave of nerves assailed her as she took in the wide hallways of the elegant, Italian Renaissance-themed hotel.

What did she think she was doing with this famous, sought-after man whose career took him all over the country, where women threw themselves at him?

Up until now, she'd avoided those fears since she hadn't fully appreciated how much of a total woman-magnet he was. But old insecurities ran deep, tied up with fears of being abandoned, fears of letting anyone get too close.

She could simply not afford to grow attached to Heath. As long as she kept her head screwed on straight, she'd be okay.

She hoped she'd be okay.

Heath had opened the door by now and he held it for her, revealing a suite that had probably been featured in world-class travel magazines. The living area where they entered was big enough to host a basketball game.

A wide, white stone chimney housed a giant flat-screen television above the hearth. A uniquely arranged bouquet of exotic flowers graced a coffee table near a basket of fruit.

"I'm panicking." She hated to be a downer, but she figured she might as well cop to the truth since they had a nice honesty thing going between them and she didn't want to blow it now for the sake of an ego that wasn't all that rock-solid anyway. "The women, the perks, the first-class... I didn't really comprehend the lifestyle even though I knew it intellectually."

Heath set down the suitcases and drew her purse off her arm to set it on a nearby stand. Divested of baggage, he took her shoulders in his hands and looked her in the eye. His Italian silk suit and understated tie bore little resemblance to the T-shirt and jeans he'd been wearing at the bar where they met. French cuffs bore links engraved with the Aces' logo and a number. His old player number?

Not in a million years would she have risked talking to him if he'd looked like this when they first met.

"We are overpaid and overprivileged," he told her. "It's not right that a man can make more than the Gross National Product of a Third World country just because he can throw a hundred-mile-an-hour fastball or hit off a left-handed pitcher. But that's the reality of the game and the value other people place on a narrow skill set. It doesn't make sense, and I know that."

"You do?" She hadn't expected him to tackle the issue head-on—and with such a self-deprecating perspective—but there it was. Groundedness. Maturity. "I can see why you make a really good manager. I'll bet it's healthy for your players to be reminded of that sometimes because this—" she gestured to the well-appointed room "—could go to people's heads."

"It can and does. And, yeah, I like to think I bring some hard-won wisdom to that dugout, but unfortunately, it takes a hell of a lot more than that to be a successful manager."

The panic eased, her worries seeming kind of superficial next to his. He really wanted this job to work, really needed it to, from what he'd explained in the cab. For him, baseball wasn't about the groupies—damn it, she of all people should know that. It meant everything to him.

"You really think you'll only get this one season to prove yourself?" She would have hated to work in a field where you had so little time to grow your talent.

"Most definitely." His hands smoothed over her shoulder and then moved lightly down her back, as if he could rub out the rest of her nervousness and transition her to another level, a tension deliciously different from the stress she'd been feeling. "The sport has the potential for big earnings, but it only rewards the smallest fraction of a percent who are at the top of their game."

"Sounds stressful."

"It takes a lot of competitive drive." His fingers rode down her spine in soft circles until she swayed closer. But then, his massage faltered and she felt him tense. "It cost me my marriage."

She straightened, curious. He'd mentioned being divorced that first night in the bar, but she hadn't been paying much attention. At the time, she'd just been relieved to know he wasn't married, given how they'd been flirting.

"What happened?" She didn't want to think about him caving to the temptations of the road. She could only imagine how aggressive the women would have been back in his playing days if they were this assertive now when he walked through a lobby with another female on his arm.

"Too much time apart. I had to be away for eighty-one games a year in twenty-six or twenty-seven different cities, give or take. Add to that the travel days to get there and back, plus sometimes heading straight from one city to another for a long stretch on the road." He shrugged and the helpless gesture made him look less like the slick manager and more like a normal guy just as confused as anyone else about how to hash out a relationship.

"She didn't want to travel with you?"

"It was too much time on the road for her. The season starts when pitchers and catchers report to spring training in the middle of February. Then, if you make the playoffs, you're playing into November. Basically, by the time I was done, she was so fed up we hardly talked over the holidays."

"That would wear on a relationship." And, not that Amber would dare to ever think about Heath in those terms, it would devastate someone like her who would always worry about infidelity and being left behind. Her own father had checked out on her, for crying out loud. What reason would she have to trust a boyfriend?

That was why she tended to go for men who approached relationships intellectually. She figured guys who looked at commitment through rational, practical eyes would be more likely to stay for the long haul.

"It did. Big-time." Heath shook his head and seemed to will away bad memories. "But I don't want to bring you down. That's been over for three years and I don't have feelings for her anymore other than regret. Besides, I brought you here to have fun."

She nodded, wondering how to separate the baggage from his past and his fame from their time together. Heck, she had a tough enough time untangling herself from Brent, apparently, since he was still calling. Not to mention, her feelings for Heath grew more complicated by the hour.

"It was all good while I was still operating under the champagne buzz from the airline service in first-class." She'd only been focused on the fun side of her impulsive decision to come with him then. Now, she felt her tendency to overthink things creeping back into her head.

"I'll bet you I can bring the buzz back." He brushed a kiss along her forehead, and the contact spurred several ideas for her.

She couldn't help but appreciate how easily he could make her whirlwind of thoughts grind to a feel-good stop. Her hands landed on the hard plank of his chest, the muscles honed from a lifetime of athleticism. She would take him at his word about what he wanted and not let anything else get in the way, damn it.

"I think I'm already humming pleasantly inside, now that you mention it."

"No more panic?" His lips hovered close to her face and she debated how best to put them in contact with her skin again.

"No. I think I hurdled past the panic to the realization that I'm alone in a hotel room with a man who holds the key to my orgasmic potential."

"Too bad I hadn't planned this better or I would have capitalized on that state of mind." He eased back, giving her time to process what his words meant.

"No quickie against the door?"

His eyes widened a fraction and she realized how much she enjoyed keeping him on his toes.

"I'm not saying no, but I did schedule a massage for you while I attend a meeting with the trainers." He checked his watch as if considering how long it would take to have her against the door.

And while she squirmed happily at the picture that painted, she was also intrigued by the alternative.

"A massage?"

"The hot stone workup is great here, but ask them for whatever you want. I figured it was the least I can do for hauling you across the country when you wanted to relax this week."

"You don't owe me anything," she protested, peering toward the window out onto a terrace with a view up

Rodeo Drive. "I haven't taken a trip farther than Nantucket in years, so just being here is a treat. But tell me this—what's your meeting about?"

She was having a hard time envisioning the full scope of his responsibilities, and his work intrigued her. He wasn't just getting paid for hitting a ball with a bat, the way she'd teased him once. She'd seen him exchange words with some of his team members back in the lobby earlier, and it struck her that Heath must have his hands full keeping that many young hotshots on track. Besides the obvious problems inherent in dealing with rookies who might be away from home for the first time and suddenly raking in millions, Heath also had to cope with the logistics of the different languages spoken in the dugout. Besides English and a few different Spanish hybrids from the Dominicans, Mexicans and so on, there was a pitching ace from Japan who couldn't communicate with any of them. Had to be tough to build team chemistry, let alone give your basic pregame pep talk.

"We need to revisit the workouts for some of our guys on the disabled list and see if we can figure out a way to keep Diego in the training room instead of on the phone with Jasmine every day. I'm really worried about him—his batting average has taken a nosedive the past two weeks, and I know he's going to be in a tailspin if he gets cut from the team."

"It's that serious?" She remembered the fans whooping it up for the third baseman at the stadium and couldn't imagine him disappearing from the game. But maybe it wasn't so rare for someone to screw up the chance of a lifetime.

Heath picked up the room keys off the dresser and gave one to her while putting the other in his pocket.

"It's like a disease in the dugout and it's infecting more players every day. Diego's swing is off, and it throws off the guy behind him in the lineup who now needs a big hit and not just a single. We're down by a few hits each game, and the pitchers start getting antsy, thinking they have to win the games with defense because the offense isn't producing. But aside from the way one guy's problems play out in a game, the effects are worse in the locker room." Heath shook his head, clearly frustrated.

"How so?"

"Diego's girlfriend had a baby and the news gets passed around the players and their girlfriends and wives. There's some jealousy from the wives who have been wanting to start families but their men have put it off because of their careers. Other players see the hell Diego is going through and bust up with their girlfriends because they've been struggling to make their relationships work, and seeing Diego get the crap kicked out of him by life only makes them more wary about getting involved. None of them want to screw up their careers."

"You guys really live in each other's back pockets that much?" It sounded more like a dysfunctional family than a team. Although they did spend a lot of time together, Amber supposed. The bonds would be tight.

"We're like a travelling fraternity." Heath checked his watch and pulled her in for a kiss. "We spend more time together than we do apart. If you ever spent three hours in a rain delay before a four-hour game, you'd know that it makes you damn close to the people waiting out the storm in that dugout with you. Good or bad, you know each other's business."

The visual created a concrete image for her and Amber thought she understood a little better. This *was* Heath's family, maybe more than the real genetic deal had been. No wonder he didn't want Diego to lose his spot on the team. He was one of Heath's own. And—to take it a step further—how crappy would it feel to get booted from your own family?

It was the position Heath sat in as much as Diego. One more reason why Heath surely fought to keep the player in the game. Knowing that about him—that he would work hard to help someone who was struggling— touched her.

"Good luck at the meeting." Winding her arms around his neck, she leaned in for a last kiss. "I'll see you back here later and you can make up for the quickie against the door."

His muscles flexed in the most interesting places in response.

"You're on." He growled the words against her ear, his mouth dipping to the sensitive place just below there to brush a kiss. "Be thinking about me when you get that massage, okay? Know that I wish it could be my hands all over you."

She tilted her head to one side to give him full access to her neck, her breath catching at the idea of stripping down and letting Heath feel her everywhere...

"Amber? Will you do that for me? Picture my hands on your hips when you're getting touched here." His palms drifted down to the curve of her waist and then edged lower. Lower. "And here."

"Mmm," she agreed, ready to shed her clothes here and now. How could he ramp up the heat between them so fast? If she'd ever felt like this with Brent, she would have known she wasn't cold.

Then again, maybe the problem had been that Brent had left her cold and she'd been too stubbornly determined to make a rational match that she hadn't seen that.

With one final kiss on her hungry lips, Heath turned and saunted out the door into the hallway. She was so hot and bothered she slumped into a boneless mass against the back of the sofa. Flustered and breathless, she hugged her arms about her waist, holding the feeling tight.

For the first time, she realized that saying goodbye to Heath at the end of the week would be more difficult than she'd ever guessed.

11

DIEGO ESTES KNEW BETTER than to hit the hotel bar.

Even as a rookie, he had an identifiable face and people tended to recognize him. Normally, he didn't mind the attention. Hell, he'd risen from the slums of the Dominican Republic to become a highly paid athlete. He still couldn't believe his good fortune to have a gift for baseball. He'd been a skinny, gawky kid with zero interest in sports, but his father had made him try out for a team when he was twelve.

Somewhere in between his old man shouting expletives from the stands and his new coach quietly explaining how to crank back his bat for the most power, Diego had fallen in love with the game. And not just because his father quit yelling for the few hours a week when Diego connected with one pitch after another. No, Diego liked baseball because it was a way he could stay out of the gangs, yet have a brotherhood all his own. The toughest gangs he'd ever run across in the D.R.

still liked baseball. Being on a team had saved Diego in a lot of ways.

He sat in the juice bar at the hotel spa, a place where a few women might hit on him, but a place where he wouldn't be recognized. At least not at a hotel in L.A. On the east coast, he might not get away with it, but in the Midwest or the west coast, the women who frequented the spa weren't expecting to meet a ballplayer downing carrot juice with ginseng. The spa towel partially draped over his head as if he were in between aromatherapy treatments helped, of course. Moving incognito through a spa was a cakewalk.

"Diego?"

The feminine voice behind him, therefore, surprised him.

Turning, he found Amber Nichols, the manager's new girlfriend. The skipper hadn't revealed much about the woman when Diego had shown up at his place the other night, but Diego had eyes. He knew Donovan was seriously hot for her.

"Hi." He gestured to the row of vacant chairs beside him and hoped the skip wouldn't castrate him if he bought her a drink. "Want to join me? I seem to be the only one in town feeling the carrot ginseng special."

"Actually—" she peered over her shoulder toward the reception desk just visible in the next room "—I do have a few minutes before my appointment."

She climbed onto the stool next to him, her long, dark braid swinging around her shoulder to brush against his. She was the kind of pretty you saw in a soap commercial. Nice skin. No makeup. A smile like she was happy inside and not trying to play head games with you.

Right now, he could really appreciate the appeal of that kind of woman.

"Any luck with Jasmine?" She pointed to the cell phone in his palm and he wondered what Donovan made of her pull-no-punches approach.

The Aces' manager wasn't exactly the kind of guy who spilled his guts for snickers and giggles.

"Nah." He couldn't even think about Jasmine without his heart going into a stop, drop and roll routine as if it sensed the need to protect itself. That shit hurt every time. "I think she's screening her calls for me. I tried from the hotel phone, too, but she must know the team is in L.A. this week." He ordered another carrot smoothie special for Amber from a spa employee who did double duty as the juice bartender and spa greeter.

Taking her drink, Amber thanked him and passed him her cell phone.

"Why don't you try calling her from mine?" She sipped the dark orange concoction experimentally. "I've got great international rates on my phone plan."

"She probably wouldn't pick up for any Boston-based number. Maybe she wouldn't pick up if I called from anywhere in the whole damn U.S."

Amber set down both the phone and her glass.

"Okay, that's way too defeatist of an attitude. First of all, she's got to talk to you sooner or later because you have a legal right to see your child." She tapped an unpolished fingernail against the smooth granite bar top. "Plus, she needs to know you want to see her and work this out, so you need to call her, her family and her friends until she gets that message. If she doesn't want anything to do with you after that, you can work out some custody with the courts, but at least you'll know you did everything you could."

She blinked at him with an earnest expression on her face and the sincerity in her voice made him feel that she knew what she was talking about. At least she had a better approach than he did, which had mostly been to drunk-dial Jasmine and tell her how much he missed her.

But maybe he didn't need to win her over to see his kid. Maybe, like Amber said, they could work out something for his son whether they were together or not.

"I don't know. I think she just flat-out hates my guts." He slumped on the juice bar, wondering where the hell his confidence had gone the past two weeks. But when even his baseball skills were in the crapper—the one thing he'd always counted on to pull him through whatever life doled out—he had to question himself.

"Get real. She had your child. She'll always be connected to you." Amber drummed her nails on the bar. "Think about it from her perspective. She's taking care of business back home while you're playing baseball for legions of adoring female fans and living it up in fancy hotels. All the groupies could give any woman a complex."

"You think?"

"Imagine how you would feel if you saw twenty guys swarm your woman for an autograph."

Diego pounded the bar and both their glasses rattled. Damn, he hated that picture.

"You talk some sense, you know that?" He took Amber's cell and dialed Jasmine's digits, thinking he could find her sister's number somewhere if she didn't answer. That sister had never liked him, but damn it, even she had to see the wisdom of letting a kid know his father.

Even if they thought he'd screw up the paternal thing, they'd have to appreciate the child care funds he wanted to contribute. His kid wasn't going to end up in a gang.

All his arguments and rationalizing disappeared, however, when Jasmine's voice answered on the other end.

"Diego, I know it's you. You can't call me every ten minutes. This phone ringing all night is going to make me lose my mind." She wasn't yelling, exactly. But it wasn't the warmest greeting he'd ever received.

Still, he enjoyed hearing the husky briskness of her voice, a voice that had whispered some really amazing things in his ear when they'd made love once upon a time. She'd always made him feel like a million bucks— long before baseball had ponied up the cash.

"Don't hang up. I need to talk to you." He tucked his head against the bar to shut out the sound of the smoothie machine mixing up a drink nearby; he didn't have to worry about Amber hearing anything because she'd already discreetly excused herself.

She hadn't even asked about getting her phone back.

For the first time in two weeks, Diego felt that he wasn't drowning in his own life. He knew he couldn't think about baseball until he had his personal stuff resolved.

On the other end of the phone, Jasmine hadn't said a word. For all he knew, she'd set the handset down and left him there to talk himself hoarse. But in the background, he heard the trill and coo of an infant and his heart puddled up inside.

"Jasmine, even if you don't want anything more to do with me, we need to at least work out something for our son's sake."

He held his breath, hoping she was there somewhere, listening. The soft sigh he finally heard might have been heavy with resignation, but after weeks of silence, it seemed like sweet music in his ears.

"Okay. But I've only got a few minutes before Alex needs a bath."

THE HOTEL ROOM was dark when Heath returned.

He'd checked out of the training meeting early, hoping to catch a glimpse of Amber in a towel down in the spa. Visions of her half-naked in the middle of a rubdown had plagued him so bad he hadn't been able to focus. But when he'd arrived in the spa, the director said she'd already been there and left, skipping out on her scheduled appointment with profuse apologies.

She didn't seem to be lying in wait for him in the hotel room, either. He hoped she would leap out at him from a darkened corner to demand her quickie against the door, but she was nowhere to be found.

When his phone rang, he expected to see her number on his caller ID. Instead, the illuminated digits belonged to his boss back in Boston. Or at least, one of his bosses. Although the team was owned jointly by several companies and individuals, the guy with the controlling share had hired him and—should the need ever arise—would be the one tasked with firing him, as well. Heath's blood temperature dropped about twenty degrees in two seconds.

"Heath Donovan," he answered, knowing Bob Tarcher III rarely made his own calls anyhow. Usually an administrative assistant contacted Heath or, if Bob needed to talk to him, the assistant got Heath on the line first.

"Heath, this is Bob. You have a minute?"

Shit. The big kahuna dialing him directly. Heath's gut sank like a high fly ball dropping in centerfield.

"Sure. Just finishing up a meeting with the trainers to evaluate some workouts. We're working with the hitting coach to see if there's anything we can tweak in Estes's swing." Might as well be straightforward about the team weaknesses. They'd been obvious enough to fans and sportswriters around the country. Thankfully, no reporters had found out about Estes's problems back home. Media glare always made that stuff worse.

"Good, good." Bob cleared his throat. "I'm calling to—hell, I don't want to be making this call at all, Heath. You know I've been behind you ever since Jeff Rally retired. But you're taking over for one of the most storied managers in baseball history. Of course that's going to invite unfair comparisons."

Heath was pretty sure his knees buckled. Something damn well buckled, because he found himself holding on to the wall like a drunkard making his way to the bar bathroom. He shook his head to clear it.

"You're axing me?" He'd been an assistant coach for one season and the manager for less than that.

"Not today, Heath. But the board met earlier in the week and they're coming down on me hard about the recent losses. You know with your inexperience, you were a controversial pick. I can only fight for you for so long."

He so did not need this now.

"Look, I appreciate the warning. Really. But I can't play every game like the guillotine is about to fall or I'm not going to build a stable foundation here." He couldn't fix Estes's problems overnight any more than he could tell the rest of the clubhouse not to worry about them. "We're dealing with some personal stuff as a team and I'm trying to help these kids, but they're young and they're rough and they don't need instability. They need consistency and help navigating rough waters."

Pulling him out of the head slot would only send

the guys reeling that much more. Not that he was such a great manager. But he was a known entity at a time when the club was really struggling to find their identity. Cohesiveness.

"Right. And I agree. I just wanted to let you know to do everything you can do to win this road stand. If you can win in L.A., I think it will buy us the rest of the season without the board breathing down our necks."

Heath shook his head. Clearly, Bob had already struck a bargain with the other owners—if the Aces won on the west coast Heath would have the team for the remainder of the season.

"Understood." Not that he liked it one damn bit. How much more pressure could he put on these guys? "But I guess I'd better get back to work if I'm going to make that happen."

They disconnected as Heath slumped down into the hotel couch, his brain turning backflips to try to figure out what he could do differently for tomorrow's game when his heart told him he shouldn't rattle the team any more. What he really wanted—needed—right now was to see Amber so he could quiet the useless second-guessing in his head. He'd never met anyone else who could divert him from baseball as well as she could. Sadly, that list included his ex-wife who had been so passionate about her job that she'd tended to get as thoroughly lost in her work as he did in his. Drawn together because they understood one another's drive, they'd quickly grown apart because their strong interests didn't leave enough time for each other.

Heath dialed Amber's cell phone, hoping that wherever she was, she could be here soon.

He damn near had a heart attack when a male voice answered her phone.

"Where's Amber?" he barked, heart slamming in his chest as if he was ready to break into a fist fight.

All that tension churning in his gut had just found an outlet.

"Skip?" the voice on the other end responded, sounding confused and appropriately wary.

He recognized the voice. The light accent.

Steam hissed from Heath's ears as he considered the implication of Diego Estes having Amber's phone. They were together? He told himself not to jump to conclusions, but life had been so damn adversarial with him lately, that proved tough to do.

"Yes," he answered tightly, slipping off his necktie before it strangled him. "Put her on the phone now."

"Whoa." Estes tried to take the laid-back approach. "Relax. Amber let me borrow her phone to call Jasmine, but your girlfriend took off before I could give it back. She left a message for me with the guy behind the juice counter at the spa before she left, though. She told him she was going to some college library. I guess she wanted me to let you know that if you called her phone."

A library? Frowning, Heath rose to his feet and strode back to the entryway of the suite. Turning on the light there, he saw a note on a stand near the basket of fresh fruit:

Had a lightbulb moment in regard to your team
and went on a run to the college library on the
UCLA campus, which stays open late. Come join
me or else I'll be back when it closes.
P.S. I let Diego borrow my phone to call the mother
of his child and apparent love of his life.
P.P.S. You're not off the hook with the quickie.

The storm inside him eased as he read the note.
Amber wasn't having a secret tryst with the third baseman. Duh. Although that twist of momentary anxiety
and fury made him better appreciate how hard it had
been for his ex-wife to deal with his fame and all the
women it brought across his path. Jealousy sucked.

"Right. Sorry, man," Heath replied lamely, knowing
his fear had been obvious in his voice when he'd asked
for Amber. But damn it, the call from the team owner
had screwed with his head. "I'm going to find her. Just
drop off her phone at the front desk, okay?"

"Sure thing, Skip. She really helped me out today,
you know? I think I've got Jasmine actually considering
making a trip up here."

Estes sounded happy. Excited. And somehow Amber
had a hand in that. Was it possible that Estes's game
would improve tomorrow because the guy had turned
some kind of corner on his personal problems?

"I'm glad for you, man. Get to bed though, okay? Big
game tomorrow and I'm counting on you."

"Right, boss. One thing, though. You ever have a girlfriend ditch you for a trip to the library before?" Estes

cracked himself up with that one before he cackled out a goodbye and hung up.

Guy was in too damn a good mood, something that hadn't happened in weeks. Heath, meanwhile, was already in the elevator and on his way down to the lobby to call a cab. He wasn't missing out on Amber for the sake of her books.

He'd been jealous to think of her with anyone else when Diego had picked up her phone. Now, all that possessiveness and the stress from the day needed an outlet.

But, oddly, he realized he wasn't just anxious to see her because he wanted to give her that massage she'd missed with his own two hands. He was also curious as hell about what she'd told Estes and what was so all-fired urgent that she needed to visit the local book mecca at nine o'clock at night.

Her note suggested she had a thought about the team.

Even though he couldn't imagine her books could provide the answers to his young team's myriad problems, he appreciated that she wanted to help save his career from going down in flames when this road trip ended.

12

A COPY MACHINE HUMMED in the background while Amber worked in the library on the UCLA campus. The sound blended with the soft whir of an excellent ventilation system that kept the books in the stacks in optimal condition. The murmur of muted study group conversations drifted occasionally to her ears. Now and then, these comforting sounds that were the same in libraries everywhere were interrupted by the high giggle or squeal of some female in the stacks.

Again, totally normal. Apparently the semiprivate nature of the floor-to-ceiling bookshelves provided enticing opportunities for grab-and-grope games on a universal basis.

It was the giggling that distracted her, reminding her that she could have stayed at the hotel and enjoyed even more private games with Heath. She only had him for such a short amount of time. What was she doing wasting precious hours with her nose in books, just like that night they'd met?

She knew the answer and didn't want to face the truth.

She was falling for Heath in spite of numerous reasons that told her it was a very bad idea. They'd only just met. He'd admitted to being bad long-term material by way of the marriage that didn't work out and his easy agreement to keep their relationship on a temporary basis. His work demanded so much from him that he had no time—or made no time—for anything else. Even if that hadn't been the case, his job would always present endless temptation in the form of female fans. How could she ever handle that with her deep-seated insecurity issues? She'd drive him away with worrying.

Then there was her job, which wasn't all that stable, either. The list went on so long she'd drive herself crazy thinking this to pieces—

"There you are."

Heath's voice sliced through the anxiety, scattering her thoughts and drawing her focus to the here and now. He strode down the aisle of tables tucked between the shelves of the biography section.

Eyes focused, jaw muscles flexed, he had looked just this same way that night she'd seen him stalk out to home plate to speak to an umpire. He appeared determined. Intense.

Ready to have his way.

A happy shiver trembled over her skin. Even knowing that being with him could be harmful to her heart, she couldn't fight the desire to take whatever happiness she could squeeze out of these few days.

"Hi." She felt breathless. Awkward.

Another muffled giggle that emanated from the rows of book nearby made heat suffuse her cheeks.

Heath didn't seem aware of the sound, however. His attention veered toward the books scattered around her. He turned two of the volumes so that the covers faced him.

"Red Auerbach. John Wooden." He turned more covers. "You've got coaching books from every sport here. Everything from NHL great Lester Patrick to baseball's own one-line king, Yogi Berra. Does this have to do with your lightbulb moment?"

"I—" She took a deep breath, willing away the strong attraction she now realized was rooted in more than the physical. As much as she'd like to hide in a hotel room with Heath for days on end, she also wanted to help him. "I could be way off base here, and you know my baseball knowledge is zilch. But I ran into Diego at the spa today."

She launched into a retelling of their conversation about the third baseman's girlfriend while Heath dropped into the seat next to her. His expression remained thoughtful, considering. Which seemed nice, given how far she'd tread out on a limb to offer an opinion on the baseball world.

"So, call me crazy," she continued, holding a high-school football coach's memoir close to her chest, "but I thought I'd go to the source for the best wisdom out there on how to develop team chemistry and motivate players. It seems like that can help win games when you've already got the necessary talent in place."

"You researched all this stuff for me?" He thumbed idly through a book of motivational quotes taken from coaches of every conceivable sport.

Amber couldn't tell if he thought she was simply being nerdy again, or if he was feeling that she'd stepped on his toes by trying to research something he'd devoted his life to. Then again, maybe he didn't think either of those things and he would see beyond the books to a depth of caring about him that she hadn't meant to reveal.

Hastily, she began stacking the resources to diminish the visual impact of the umpteen volumes scattered everywhere.

"I'm a bookworm. It's what I do." Too late, she realized her actions had uncovered a legal pad full of notes in longhand.

Amber Nichols, geek extraordinaire.

Heath's hand darted to hers, stilling her efforts to clean up the area.

"This is really great of you. I've meant to read a lot of these at different points in my career, but never made the time."

His eyes conveyed a sincerity that melted her heart and made her realize she was toast when it came to this man. How had she let this happen?

"It was nothing—"

He kissed her, staunching the flow of words with the tender barrier of his lips. Awareness flamed to life, flicking over her skin to tantalize every inch of her with wanting. Her eyelids drifted closed, her senses narrowing to focus on Heath's scent and touch. She breathed him in, letting the moment burn away the awkwardness, the worries and the burden of too many thoughts.

He pulled away from her so slightly that she did not even bother to open her eyes.

"It's *not* nothing," he whispered, his thumb roaming over the back of her hand in a sweet, subtle stroke. "It's something no one else would have thought to do for me and something I really needed tonight."

She forced her eyes open at the vehemence—the pure conviction—in his voice. Happiness warmed her heart for a moment and then her attention snagged on the last part of what he'd just said.

"What do you mean? Did something happen?" She could tell something must have gone wrong.

"The team owner called after the meeting. He said they're giving me run of the team for this road series, but if I can't win in L.A., I'm done."

"You can't be serious." Her eyes were wide-open now, the electric hum in her skin short-circuiting at the news. "That's like my department editor saying I have to sell a few thousand more papers to keep writing my column."

How incredibly unfair.

Behind them, an assistant librarian strode through the floor announcing they would be closing shortly.

"Well, it's done." Heath squeezed her hand tighter. "I can't make any radical changes to my game plan at this point, but who knows? Maybe I can light a fire under these guys in the locker room thanks to your help."

He gestured toward her piles of notes and books. Never in her life had her academic approach felt as small as right at that moment. He was being unfairly railroaded, and there wasn't a damn thing she could do to help.

"I had so many ideas. I thought the players' wives and girlfriends would get together more. I thought you could get some more translators for a night out—"

"And maybe I'll have the chance to try all of that." Rising from the chair, he scooped up her bag and notes. "I'll sure as hell look over some of this before I hit the locker room tomorrow, but right now there's only one thing that will make this better."

"A breach of contract lawsuit."

"No." With his free hand, he tugged her toward the elevator. "Sex all night long. And the sooner the better."

Her heart tripped over itself even more than her suddenly stumbling feet.

"Oh." She looked back with longing at the high shelves of books that hid lovers among the stacks. "I know somewhere we could go just to, er, take the edge off."

HE'D BEEN TEMPTED.

Amber had glanced toward the towering racks with a mischievous gleam in her eyes, twirling her braid between her fingers like a naughty co-ed bent on getting into trouble. It was the last thing he'd expected from her, and he'd bet his World Series ring that she'd never tried something like that before. Which, of course, had made him all the more eager to take her back there and fulfill every fantasy.

But a public indiscretion could have him booted out of the clubhouse before tomorrow's game even got under way, so he'd opted to pay the cab driver double to deliver them back to their hotel quickly.

Now, he sat beside her in the darkened backseat of a yellow taxi while the driver sped down Sunset Boulevard.

"I can't believe I missed out on a chance like that." Heath breathed in the scent of her shampoo where he'd already started to unwind the braid. The layers of hair inside were still slightly damp even though he'd bet she'd showered hours ago. "If I get fired tomorrow and my public image no longer matters, you have to promise me you'll go back to that library with me."

"No way." She ducked her head against his shoulder and rubbed her cheek against his chest. "I can't believe I proposed something so outrageous in the first place. It's just that I've heard couples fooling around in the stacks in libraries a million times. Maybe it's a rite of passage for academic types."

Other cars honked as their cab extricated itself from a knot of traffic.

"Damn it." Heath could picture her working diligently in nameless libraries around Boston, trying to ignore the sounds of couples sneaking a feel nearby. "I deprived you of something you could have thought about every time you're in a library for the rest of your life."

And knowing Amber's love of books, that would be a lot of times.

"Why don't you make it up to me by providing what I've *really* wanted all evening?"

As the cab drew to a stop in front of the hotel, he racked his brain to think what that would be.

"The massage?" He hated to give her up for that long, but this was supposed be her vacation.

One of the hotel valets opened the taxi's door while Heath paid the driver. Amber's half-undone hair slid forward over one shoulder as she stepped out of the cab and peered back at him.

"The quickie."

Hallelujah.

Heath turned to the valet still holding the cab door while Amber walked toward the hotel a few paces ahead of him.

"The front desk has my girlfriend's cell phone. Could you send it up to Room 5163 in about an hour?" He passed the kid a ten. Then dug in his wallet for a second. "Actually, make that two hours, and could you tell room service to bring something then, too? Good red wine and a pizza?"

"Of course, Mr. Donovan." The kid nodded, hiding any smirk he might have had at overhearing Amber's mention of a quickie. "And I'll be rooting for you tomorrow. I'm from Hartford."

"Good man." Heath slapped him on the back. "We'll need some fans on our side."

He hurried to catch up to Amber, wanting to touch her so he wouldn't think about that damn game anymore. As much as he appreciated hearing from the Aces' fans, he couldn't worry about things he couldn't control. His best pitcher wouldn't be ready to pitch until the following game, so they had to go with a new guy they'd just pulled up from the minors. The bullpen had been struggling all year since they had no depth in that department— *No*. He shut down that line of thinking, jogged through the hotel doors that a bellhop held open for him and hurried past the front desk.

At the elevator bank, Amber stood inside an empty car, one finger pressing a button on the control panel.

"Going up?" A smile teased one side of her lips. She'd lost the tie in her hair somewhere between the cab and the hotel, so now the waves spilled free over the shoulders of her simple cotton dress.

"Hell, yes."

He barged in the elevator and dragged her finger away from the button that held the doors open. He didn't wait for them to close behind her, but backed her up against the rear wall, his hands on her waist.

She went willingly. Eagerly. Shrugging her purse strap off her shoulder, she let it fall to the floor and then wrapped her arms around his neck. He pulled her hips to his, sealing them together.

"You forgot to hit the button for the fifth floor," she

whispered, arching her neck as if she wanted a kiss there.

"I know exactly what to hit to take you where you want to go." He breathed the words along her skin before he took a sample taste.

Her soft whimper vibrated against his lips and hummed along his tongue. He could feel the thrum of her pulse at her throat and the need to have her naked seized him hard.

"Hurry," she urged, untwining an arm from his neck to reach for the elevator buttons.

Some part of his brain told him they were probably at the penthouse level by now. Thank God no one else had wanted a ride yet. He leaned back enough so she could reach the button for their floor.

Ding!

The elevator chimed as it slowed to a stop—on the sixth floor instead of the fifth.

"Stay in front of me." Heath moved Amber to stand between him and entrance, unable to gain control of himself before the sliding doors hissed open.

He kept his arms wrapped around her waist and ducked his chin to kiss her shoulder.

"Hey, Skip." The Aces' big-money closer, Chase Montoya, stepped into the cabin with star pitcher Jay Cannon.

Clearly dressed for a night on the town, Jay's black silk shirt and black pants made him look like stereotypical New York mafia while Montoya's baseball jersey and gold necklace as thick as a climbing rope were more suited to a rap video.

"You guys aren't setting a bad example for my rookies by blowing off curfew, are you?" Heath wished he could put Amber under his arm and hide her from view since these two gawked at her as if they'd never seen a woman before.

She did look hot as hell with her cheeks all flushed and her lips swollen from his kisses. And that hair—so long and wavy—made her look like some lush, mythical goddess.

"I'm not due on the mound tomorrow, boss," Jay clarified, though they all knew that Chase would be tapped for a save if the Aces got a lead. "Tonight, we figured we'd hit the bars for a celebrity hunt."

With Montoya a veteran earning the big bucks, Heath let it go. As a player, he'd never appreciated being told how to prepare for games. But damn it, these guys set a bad example for the new and impressionable types.

"Just stay away from fans with videophones, all right? I don't need to see you two on TMZ highlights tonight." Heath wondered if he'd even be employed by the team on Saturday when it was Jay's turn to pitch.

Ding!

The car arrived at their floor, and Amber wrapped her arms around him.

"Night!" she called to them as Heath escorted her out of the elevator and down the hall to his suite.

Nothing else was getting in the way of what he

wanted now. No players. No meetings. No phone calls threatening his job.

"I'm bolting the door and throwing my phone across the room," he warned her, inserting his key card into the lock. "No more interruptions. No more trips to the library."

"Really?" She crossed the threshold as he held open the door. "What if I have a sudden urge to consult a book?"

He followed her inside and slid the bolt into place. Blue lights from above the bar were the only illumination, except for the glow from the street below that filtered in under partially closed blinds. The lights from Rodeo Drive remained bright long after the stores closed.

He regretted that she hadn't gotten to see anything of the city so far, but that was what his life was like on the road—hotels and ball fields.

"I'm going to teach you everything you'll need to know. No books necessary." He stepped deeper into the room and shrugged off his suit jacket.

Loosened his tie.

Her eyes followed the movement of his hand on the knot before her gaze tracked back up to his face.

"But I like being an expert on things," she persisted, though she was already stepping out of her shoes. Her purse hit the bar with a thud.

"Guess I'll have to send you straight to the master class."

He reached for her, and she was in his arms in a

heartbeat. Quick, clever fingers fluttered all over his chest, dipping between shirt buttons to unfasten them.

"Less talk. More naked." She yanked his shirt backward off his shoulders and nearly strangled him with his tie. "Oh!"

She reached to loosen it more, but he beat her to the knot.

"I've got it." He tossed the neckwear with all the power of a centerfielder going straight to the plate.

"I told you I need my reference manuals," she reminded him, placing a kiss on the hot skin of his chest.

The soft curve of her breasts teased him through the fabric of her cotton dress. She was so sexy in her classic, simple clothes and her practical braid. Not femme fatale heels and knock-him-out perfume. Amber was beautiful for not trying. And just what he needed to keep his mind off tomorrow's game. This was more than a good idea. It was a damn great idea.

"One day when we're not in a hurry, I'll give you a step-by-step tutorial," he assured her. "Right now, we're going to fast-forward through all that."

"No instructions?"

"No more fighting with the clothes. We can work around the rest." He picked her up and backed her against the door they'd just entered. He gripped her bare thighs beneath her dress, but she wrapped her legs so hard around him, he could have let go and she wouldn't have fallen.

A gasp rose from her lips. She clutched his shoulders and made sexy little sounds that drove him crazy.

"I've wanted this all day." His thumbs speared beneath the lace of her panties, claiming the new terrain of unbelievably soft skin.

Silky damp curls hid her slick heat, but he sifted his way through to touch the tender bud of her sex. Wet with wanting, her body wept for him in the sweetest sign of feminine desire.

Heat fired through him, his whole body a hot, hard ache. He didn't just want Amber. He needed her with a fierceness that rocked him.

The drive to be inside her—to give and take, pleasure and possess—was so strong he unfastened his pants and nudged his boxers aside. He was beyond ready.

"Condom," a voice of reason murmured. Her voice. "Please say you restocked."

It took him a moment to realize she was digging through his pants pocket for a reason. A damn good one, at that. When had he ever lost control so badly that he never even thought about protection?

She emerged from the pocket with the necessary item and lost no time ripping open the packet with her teeth. Her one-handed effort to slide the condom on him was a teeth-clenching exercise in restraint, but he managed to hold back until she guided him toward the slick feminine heat between her legs.

The urge to explain himself—that he couldn't slow down because he'd never felt like this before—died in his throat. He gripped her thighs, drawing her closer to edge his way deeper.

Burying his face in the cascade of hair over her shoulder, he inhaled the scent of her. Soap and flowers. Sex and desire.

For a long moment, he just held her there, acclimating to the feel of her. Relishing the fact that he'd gotten lucky enough to find her that night at The Lighthouse.

"I'm so close," she whispered, her voice thin and sweet in the darkness broken only by the blue bar light. "It feels so good."

Heath thrust and watched her through half-opened eyes, her head tossing back and forth as if she were in the throes of a dream she didn't want to end. Raw masculine pride surged through him that he did that to her.

And suddenly, it was all too much.

He held her steady, burying himself inside her over and over again as his release blindsided him. Amber held on tight, her nails finding purchase in his shoulders for a moment before she shuddered and contracted all around him.

Nothing else mattered but her. This moment.

Their bodies slick with heat and sex, they dissolved together in a boneless heap and he was damn lucky he didn't drop her. Forcing one foot in front of the other, he stalked through the suite to the bedroom with her in his arms. They collapsed onto the pristine navy comforter, surrounded by pillows and bolsters.

For once, baseball didn't come rushing back to his

brain in the quiet moment when his body was satiated. It was there in the background, but he could separate himself from it, and for that, he was damn glad.

"You're amazing." He couldn't begin to analyze the way she'd gotten into his head and stayed there.

She'd crashed into his life, not looking where she was going, and that had turned out to be the best accident that had ever happened to him.

"Maybe it should be me teaching the master class after all," she murmured, rubbing her cheek on his shoulder like a contented cat.

Like someone who cared about him.

The warmth of the moment fractured a little at the realization. Funny that it wasn't baseball that did it, but his own fear of hurting her. Of disappointing her.

His gut clenched at the thought.

Ruthlessly, he ignored the niggling concern, knowing he couldn't think about that now with her lying beside him. She'd come to him with too many old worries about sex for him to get wrapped up in his head now. She deserved to have him wax poetic about how fantastic she was.

"All that book smarts must be paying off," he agreed, vowing he would not let himself hurt her. Even if that meant he'd have to let her go sooner than what he wanted. Reaching for her, he rubbed her hip and realized he'd never undressed her. A fact which he would remedy immediately. "But I think we'll need to test your skills one more time before you're awarded that designation."

"Knute Rockne said we should build up our weaknesses until they become our strong points." She helped him untangle her bra straps from her clothes so he could reveal every smoking hot inch of creamy flesh.

"Bring it on, Professor," he replied.

It was going to be so damn hard not to fall for her.

13

"I CAN SEND A PLANE down there right now and you could be watching my game tonight." Diego cradled the hotel phone against his ear at one o'clock in the morning, grateful to have Jasmine on the other end of the line after so many failed attempts to reach her over the past two weeks.

"Forget it. I'm not some spoiled socialite who needs a private jet and a designer purse with a cross-breed dog the size of a rodent," she protested, stringing her words together in a whispered rant out of deference to their sleeping son.

Damn but she was a good mom.

He could picture her in the condo he'd helped her move into after college so she could be close enough to the local rec center to walk to her job. She'd worked hard to obtain a four-year degree as a counselor in three years. And he'd known she would be great at setting wayward kids straight since she was the most no-nonsense, get-your-act-together person he'd ever met.

Jasmine had always been the practical problem solver. He'd been the dreamer.

"I would never try to make you into someone you're not. I respect you and the way you see the world. You encourage people to look beyond themselves to make it a better place." He hoped he'd said that right. He didn't want to waste his one chance. "But there's nothing wrong with wanting to be with you right now. And you've got to know I can't wait to meet Alex."

His throat burned if he thought about it too much—that he'd missed his son's first weeks. Diego punched the overstuffed hotel pillow next to his head to try to make a dent, but the thing exploded right back into shape.

"I *do* want him to know you." Jasmine's quiet admission surprised him. Up until now, she'd only defended her right to raise the child on her own since Diego had left, according to her, without a backward glance.

Which had been true. But damn it, he hadn't possessed all the facts.

"You have a damn funny way of showing it. You could have called me. Or told my mom." Diego had moved his mother to southern Florida after his father died last year. "You know my mom would have been so happy."

"Have you told her?" Jasmine diverted the underlying question, but he didn't mind.

As long as she came here, Diego didn't care about the rest.

"No." He flipped the pillow, hoping the other side would be more accommodating than the rest of his screwed-up life. "Can you imagine if I told her she had a grandson and the boy wasn't right there for her to kiss and hug and spoil? I'd never hear the end of it. When I tell her, it's going to be with you at my side and a kid in hand."

"I'll bet your mom has had a hard year with you being away all the time."

"She's living in the nicest house in Coral Gables." Did she think he wouldn't take care of his own mother?

"Mmm."

She didn't say anything about the house, but he could tell he'd somehow screwed that up, too, although how a guy could go wrong buying his mother a sweet-ass house with a hot tub and a security gate, he didn't know. He was about to ask, but she filled the quiet space with an observation of her own.

"She lost her husband right when she was trying to get used to you being in the States. And while I know you had good intentions moving her to Florida, I'm sure she's a little homesick for the Dominican Republic. She has so many friends here." Jasmine made sympathetic sort of noises that made him feel less as if she was blaming him. "What's all that noise on your end?"

He stilled in between the blows he delivered to the crappy piece of foam that had become his worst enemy. The damn thing wasn't like the ones back home, just like nothing else in his life was the same as it used to be.

"I can't get comfortable with these hotel pillows." It was a small thing, but damn.

Her squeal of laughter on the other end surprised him.

"Oh, God, I can picture that. You only like those squirrelly down pillows once there's no feathers left inside." More laughter. "Why don't you travel with yours in your suitcase? It wouldn't take up more room than a pair of jeans, knowing how you like a pillow."

He tossed the foam imposter onto the floor and balled up the bedsheet to put under his head instead. He felt better—not just because of the sheet solution. But because he had Jasmine laughing that big, brassy laugh in his ear, keeping him real and solving problems in ways he wouldn't have thought of if he traveled for ten more years.

"Were you born knowing everything, woman?" He wasn't about to let her discover she could buy and sell his heart three times over. Not when she could still hang up the phone and shut him out of her life again.

"Not even close." Her sigh put him on alert. Something was bothering her.

"Why do you say that? What's wrong?" Diego might suck at fixing his own problems, but he would make sure hers went away.

She was a good person and she deserved life to be easier a whole lot more than he did. Too bad working with kids and keeping them out of harm's way in the inner city didn't pay nearly as much as baseball.

"There's a lot I don't have figured out, Diego. Starting with how I'd deal with the fame if I got involved in your life again."

She was actually considering it? That was the best freaking news he'd had in weeks. No. Honestly, it was the best news he'd had all year. He'd missed having her around to keep him grounded. To call him on it when he let success go to his head. To help him ward off false friends who only wanted to borrow money or cash in on his career. Beyond that, he missed the down-to-earth reality of a woman who was more concerned with living a happy life than keeping up appearances.

"Baby, the fame has some perks that can make your life easier."

"Like your mama's big house in Coral Gables? I don't want to be stashed away in some cold mansion and wait around for you to visit twice a year, thank you very much."

Damn. He remembered what Amber had said about the fame—well, actually, the abundance of available females—giving a woman a complex. Maybe that was part of what was bugging Jasmine.

"You and Alex could travel with me," Diego assured her, already picturing how different his hotel room would look if there was a playpen on one side of his bed and Jasmine lying right next to him. His heart hurt just thinking how much better he'd like that. "You both can be with me every minute I'm not on the field. And it's not like in the minors where we travel on buses and stay in crap places. We'd have the money for a nanny and direct flights first-class—anything that would make it easier for you."

"A nanny?" She sounded indignant, but amused at

the same time. "Wait until you see this baby of yours. You won't ever want to give him up long enough to hand him over to anyone else."

His heart did that aching thing again.

"Let me see." His voice went all hoarse and he had to clear his throat before he could continue. "Go take a picture and send it to me on the phone."

"Okay." She made some rustling noises and he heard a door creak on her end. "It might be a little dark, but I can't turn on the light."

"It's okay." Diego lay back down, wondering if he could convince her to stay on the phone all night. He couldn't go back to that place he'd been the past two weeks—running around like a jackass, taking nips from a flask and hitting the skipper's security gate. What would she think of him if she knew about that?

"There," she whispered. The creaking noise returned and he pictured her leaving the nursery. "I'm sending it now. You can check your e-mail in a second."

He listened to her messing with the phone buttons as he stared out the open blinds at the lights from Rodeo Drive below. Los Angeles held no appeal for him without her. Without his family.

"Jasmine, I need you to be here for tomorrow's game." So much was riding on it. Heath hadn't said as much, but Diego knew the higher-ups were breathing down his neck.

Diego also knew a lot of that was his fault. He had to pull himself out of this slump.

"I don't know, Diego. I don't want to be the woman

who holds you back from achieving your dreams. That was the main reason I had to set you free the first time. I knew you were too big to stay here and I wasn't ready to leave home."

He digested her words and the idea of her "setting him free" so he could chase his dreams instead of her dumping him. Was that really how she saw it?

"My dreams aren't all that fun without you." He put the phone on speaker so he could tap his way through to his e-mail.

"They say you're a ladies' man now." Her voice was formal, with no trace of the warmth or the laughter that had been there before.

"Jasmine." He wondered how to address that and figured the best response was the truth. "It hurt like hell when you broke up with me. I only dated a lot of women because I could tell after one dinner out that they didn't come close to you."

He heard a little sigh from her on the other end of the phone and he thought maybe he'd made some small amount of headway. God, he regretted hurting her. He'd make damn sure it didn't happen again.

"I'm a single mom, you know. I can't afford to get my heart broken, or worse, have you get close to our son and break his heart, too."

Just then, he found the e-mail in his inbox. His gut clenched. He clicked it open.

"Oh, my God." Diego stared at the picture of the sleeping baby with a Spider-Man pajama top snapped on little red shorts that showed off chubby legs. Little Alex gripped the ear of a terry-cloth rabbit with one hand, while the other rested by his mouth, as if he'd just quit sucking a thumb. Diego felt his heart damn near burst out of his chest. "That's our boy."

"Yeah." Her voice went soft again and he could hear maternal pride radiating from eight thousand miles away. "He sure is."

A new, scary sense of responsibility made him a little light-headed. He was a father. He was responsible for that scrap of life. His hand gravitated toward the screen to stroke the swirls of dark curls on the boy's head. He knew being responsible called for more than just putting a roof over his head and teaching him how to throw a ball; Diego had to make sure that he had reasons to smile.

"I'm opening a bank account for him—for you both—tomorrow before the game." His son would have anything he needed. Diego's priorities had reshuffled so fast he could hardly process all the things he needed to take care of. "You're letting me help you out, Jasmine. I'm going to be down there to help you raise him every day that I have off. And I'm sending open-ended plane tickets so you can be here any time you want. I understand if you're not ready yet. But I'm willing to wait until you see that I'm not going anywhere and I'm not giving up on you or him."

"Okay." Her word was so soft he almost talked right over it.

"What?" He paused in the middle of zooming in on the baby's face. "Okay what?"

"Okay, go ahead and send your chartered flight down here tonight if it really won't break the bank. I can get tomorrow off from the center. Alex and I will come see you for a few days, and I'll see for myself how serious you are."

He nearly dropped his laptop as he sprang off the bed, instantly alert as if he'd chugged two Red Bulls.

"Seriously?"

"Call me a sucker for the father of my child." Her voice was a little breathless and he hoped like hell that meant she was excited to see him, too. "But yes. I can't wait for you to meet him. And we'll just…see what happens."

Happiness exploded in his chest like the fireworks after a grand slam for the home team. His hand was shaking like a rookie's in his first plate appearance as he reached for his laptop to set the wheels in motion.

"You won't regret this." He would be awake all night making arrangements, but he would ensure everything was perfect for her.

He just hoped he could put the bat on the ball tomorrow since he wouldn't get much sleep. But with his son and the woman he loved on their way to see him, he couldn't find it in his heart to care.

"I COULD GET USED to this." Amber chased her slice of wood-fired pizza with a sip of mellow Chianti from her perch against the pillows in the hotel bed. "The wine really goes with the red sauce."

Room service had delivered her phone along with

the food, providing the perfect dinner in bed to cap off a really incredible night with Heath.

"Yeah, but what's with the goat cheese?" Heath eyed his third slice suspiciously, though the wariness didn't seem to diminish his appetite. "I'm a purist when it comes to pizza."

"Must be a west coast thing." She tipped her head against the smooth, polished headboard and admired the view out the partially opened blinds. Their hotel was taller than most of the nearby buildings, so there was little danger of anyone looking back at them.

Heath seemed very careful about protecting his privacy from camera lenses, which fit with what she'd learned about him after their very first night together. He would never be the kind of guy who sought the spotlight and that felt reassuring to a woman who occasionally grappled with insecurity.

"I can't believe I got you room service for dinner on your first night in Beverly Hills." He moved the box off the bed and swiped away the crumbs. "You deserved to see more of the city."

"Not just room service." She pointed to the advertisement on the pizza box. "It's the best pie in town. Besides, if you started to wine and dine me, I'd have major culture shock and might go running back home. Midnight snacks during the late show are right up my alley."

She'd been out of her element at the spa today—no doubt that had been one of the reasons she'd followed her nose to the local library on the first excuse she'd found. She hadn't just been helping out Heath with her research about creating a healthy team psychology. She'd been running to a place of comfort in a world shifted far off-kilter.

"That's my world, too, most nights." He refilled his glass with the dark red wine, but she declined more. If the room started spinning tonight, she wanted it to be because she was seeing stars from the way Heath made her feel, and not because she'd gotten carried away on Chianti.

"So you said your ex-wife wasn't interested in traveling with you?" She wanted to know more about the marriage that hadn't worked out for him. Not because she was nosy but she couldn't imagine a woman giving up on him so fast. And maybe she secretly wondered if he still had feelings for her. "I'm surprised she didn't at least try that the next baseball season instead of walking away after just one year."

"She said my job shouldn't be more important than hers, and I could see her point." He shrugged, his shoulder brushing hers as he slumped back against the headboard with her, gazing out at the city lights and the low rooftops of the buildings nearby.

A few streets over, she spotted a hotel or maybe a nightclub with a pool on the roof surrounded by palm trees and late-night partiers.

"But marriage is about compromise." Or it should be. In her parents' marriage, her mother had done all the compromising, and it still hadn't been enough to keep her father faithful.

"That was her point exactly. She said she'd travel with me for half the year if I'd travel with her for half the year. But since baseball demands more like three quarters of a year, I wasn't holding up my end."

"She must have known that when she met you."

"Well, if either of us had been planners or thinkers like you, we would have had that mapped out ahead of time." He clinked his glass next to hers and took a drink, as if toasting her worst trait—overthinking. "But since she was more like me with that 'I know what love is when I see it' kind of attitude, we flew into the unknown without really figuring out how it would all work. And it didn't."

So they gave up?

As much as the outcome of that story seemed frustrating from a romantic's standpoint, Amber appreciated the ending, given that his divorce had allowed her to meet him in the first place. Heath Donovan was so different from any other guy she'd ever dated. What had started out as a big risk for her was rewarding her many times over. Pizza and Chianti in bed was only the beginning.

"What about you? Didn't you plan for a future with Brent?" He set her empty glass aside along with his and then dragged her down to lie beside him, their heads sharing a pillow.

He even edged back a little to make sure she had enough room in a gesture that squeezed her heart.

"I did plan on a future, right down to where we would live and where we could vacation that would be halfway between my mother's house and his parents' place so that our families could spend quality time with us every year." She felt embarrassed thinking about it now—like a high-school girl coloring in her initials next to her boyfriend's on a notebook. "But you can't plan to fall in love with someone. And just because you'd like it to happen doesn't mean it will."

Heath was silent for a long moment. Then he leaned closer to brush a kiss along the top of her head.

"My father always tried to tell me I didn't plan enough—in life or in baseball. His big motto is See The Whole Field. But I never understood how you could plan for things when you never knew if the next pitch would be a curveball. You can only work with what you're given, and most of the time, you don't have any damned control over what that will be."

Amber knew he was right, but she hated to think she had so little input on her future.

"Will your dad come to the game tomorrow?" Idly kissing Heath's shoulder, she wondered how she'd ever go back home to the isolated nights in her apartment after the days and nights she'd known with him.

Would she ever get to meet Diego's girlfriend? Or enjoy being by Heath's side when his team was on a winning streak and his job was secure?

"Front and center. As a former L.A. star, he's able to command the best seats."

"Is that weird?" It was a vague question, but she was curious about the family dynamic.

Even though Heath said he'd forgiven his father

for not being a part of his life—for not accepting him until he proved his worth on the baseball field—Amber sensed a strained relationship at best.

"Maybe. Yes." He stroked through her hair, twining it around his fingers, back and forth. "It's tough to be your best in front of someone who only seems to see your shortcomings."

"Will I meet him?" She didn't know if that was pushy. After all, most guys didn't introduce their girlfriends to their parents unless it was serious.

But she was stuck to Heath's side while she was in L.A., so they might run into his dad whether or not Heath meant for it to happen.

"Probably. If you want to." He stopped weaving her hair and she peered up at him to see him frowning. "Amber?"

"Yes?" She tensed, reading some sort of reservation—a guardedness—in his expression.

"If we lose tomorrow, I'm not sticking around town to meet with the higher-ups and take the ax in person." The grim set to his mouth told her that he considered this a real possibility. "I don't want to ruin your vacation, but it will be a PR nightmare for the team and for me, too."

"Won't it be even worse for you in Boston?" She worked for a newspaper. She knew exactly how much interest a change in management for Boston's baseball team would generate. The guys in the sports department would work around the clock, literally, to exhaust the news value of that story online and in print.

Too soon, she'd be right back in the thick of that endless pressure herself, a thought she'd stuffed to the furthest recesses of her brain these past few days. It wasn't healthy to feel so much anxiety about a job—hers, or his, either.

"I don't think I'd return to Boston. At least not right away." His eyes were fixed on some distant, invisible point out the hotel window and she felt a gap a mile wide open up between them. "I couldn't even go to the beach house on Nantucket. Too many reporters know to look for me there."

"So..." She waited for him to spell out what that meant for her. When his brooding look never changed, she thought she'd better pin down some clarification. "You'd like me to return to Boston on my own, then."

She hoped that wasn't what he meant. And yet...he didn't answer very quickly.

His gaze flickered back to her, his hand still woven through her hair like a forgotten project.

"Only if we lose." Gently, he untangled his fingers. "I hope you know I never expected I'd receive this kind of ultimatum when I asked you to come here with me."

She felt a little shell-shocked at the realization that her time with him would be over—for good—if his team lost tomorrow. Intellectually, she knew he had to feel even more adrift than her since he'd put his whole life into baseball and he could lose it in the course of a game. Still, it was clear that Heath didn't have the sense of attachment to her that she'd developed for him over the past few days.

Months ago, Brent's defection and parting jab had made her question everything she thought she knew about love and dating. Sure it had hurt. But now, she understood that Brent had mainly wounded her pride— she hadn't really loved him.

Amber might not have realized that at the time. But now she knew for sure. What she'd felt for Brent was a pale facsimile of the emotions she'd experienced with Heath.

Emotions she would not name—even in the privacy of her own head—to save herself from admitting to a feeling that would only devastate her.

"Amber?" Heath's voice prodded her for a response, reminding her that he was waiting for her to relinquish any claim to him this week so he could leave town if the need arose.

No muss. No fuss.

"Of course, I understand." It was the truth, since she was an expert at thinking through things and she could fully appreciate that Heath would have few professional options after tomorrow's game if he lost his job. "It makes sense to avoid the Aces' backyard for a while."

Her heart burned even more than her eyes as she said what he wanted to hear. Hadn't she promised herself to date for fun and not get caught up in romanticizing things? But damn it, Heath wasn't like the other guys she'd dated. She herself wasn't the same person she'd been the week before. Knowing him had opened up a new side of her that she hadn't known she possessed.

Someone bolder and more adventurous. Someone who had a world of knowledge to share.

Her heart ached at the thought of all she'd lose tomorrow if the Aces lost.

And if they won?

She'd only be putting off the inevitable. Los Angeles had been her fairy-tale world where all things were possible. No matter when she returned to Boston, she would be alone once that plane touched the tarmac.

Heath couldn't have been any more clear.

"Right." He appeared relieved that she understood. "But I'd make sure you got back to Boston, first-class and whenever you want. I can make all the arrangements for you, even if I need to leave right from the ballpark."

The pizza that had tasted so good a few minutes ago churned uneasily in her gut. He would really do that? Jet right out of that ball field like a stranger to her and leave her on her own to pack and get to the airport?

The chill of that potential non-goodbye opened her eyes to what little held them together. Or, rather, what compelled *him* to stay with her.

Absolutely nothing beyond the physical.

A gaping hole opened up in her chest, and it was all she could do not to clutch the spot with both hands.

"Don't worry about it," she reassured him, her mouth on autopilot since her heart was currently six feet under and her brain had shut off in protest. "I can make my own plans to return home if that happens."

And damn it, either way now—win or lose—she

would make her own travel plans home. Like him, she didn't want to stick around and wait for the ax to fall. She would help him get through the game tomorrow because—whether he knew it or not—he needed her. She had something to offer and if he was too thick-headed to recognize that, she wasn't about to chase after him to make him see the obvious.

Yes, her heart hurt like hell, but she deserved better.

"No, Amber, it's my fault you're here." He punctuated it with a kiss that failed to reassure her. "I'll take care of everything and make sure you return home safely. I'm not going to let my career ruin your week, as well."

Too late. It already had.

14

HEATH WAS OFF HIS GAME today and couldn't quite figure out why. Nerves, he could understand. But his brain was in some kind of mental fog that he couldn't shake.

He'd slid out of bed before dawn to seek coffee in a quiet corner of the hotel. Now he sat at a small table between the gift shop and a croissant cart, sucking down an espresso while trying to sift through the flotsam junking up his head.

Yes, he could be facing the end of his career. That would rattle anyone. But he also kept thinking about Amber back in the hotel room and how he'd pushed her away prematurely. He'd known the whole idea of not wanting to wreck her vacation had been B.S. Preparing her for the inevitable had felt wrong even though he had damn good reasons. At the start of the night, he'd been so grateful to be with her that he didn't think about his impending career doom. Then he'd robbed himself of that happiness, convinced he'd screw up with her the same way he'd messed up with the Aces.

"Heath?" A familiar gravelly voice cut into his thoughts.

He looked up to find a grizzled old baseball hero peering down at him, still wearing an L.A. Stars jersey twenty-five years after he'd retired from the game.

"Dad." Heath used one foot to nudge forward the chair opposite him before he rose to clap his dad on the shoulder in a sorta-hug Heath reserved for him alone. "Have a seat."

The man frowned as he took off his cap and set it on the table before sliding into the chair.

"You don't look surprised to see me." Mark Donovan still worked out five days a week and maintained his athlete's build.

Fans of all ages frequently recognized him, and Heath's father seemed to like that quite a bit. Mark Donovan hadn't just been a player. He'd been a sports superstar, crushing fastballs into the third tier of baseball stadiums around the country before a knee injury had finished his playing days.

Even now, he seemed to expect a ticker tape parade wherever he went and, frankly, Heath wasn't up for it today.

"No, I'm not surprised to see you around." Heath had half expected his father to show up at the hotel yesterday since the Major League Baseball schedule was made public well in advance of the season and Mark knew where the Aces preferred to stay when they came to town. Besides, Mark shared Heath's habit of waking early to scout out caffeine. "I figured you'd have some words of wisdom before the curtain falls on my managing career."

Heath had just hoped he could have received them in a voice mail or a text message.

Across the table, his father signaled to the woman behind the croissant kiosk and asked for a latte. Heath didn't bother telling him this wasn't a sit-down restaurant since the lady hurried over with a tall cup and a wink for him.

"You don't really think they're serious about cutting you loose after less than one season?" At least his father did him the credit of sounding genuinely shocked.

"I've been put on notice that if we lose this road series, I'm out."

"Son of a—"

"Exactly. But right from the start it was apparent that anyone taking over for the legendary Jeff Rally in Boston would be screwed." Heath had weighed the consequences, knowing the Hall of Fame–bound coach who'd put twenty years into the team would be a tough act to follow. But maybe failure wasn't something he'd ever really seriously considered.

Now, it seemed as if he was facing defeat on every front, including his relationship with Amber.

What if today was the end of everything for him? Would she really fly back to Boston alone?

Around them, a few early-morning risers were whispering and pointing at the father-son baseball pair and while he didn't ever mind meeting with fans, it might have been nice if his dad had skipped the team jersey for their impromptu family breakfast.

"Any manager needs more time than that." Heath's father sipped his latte thoughtfully.

"It's not a one-man show in the owner's office anymore. Bob has to answer to a board." There didn't seem to be any way around that.

Mark nodded, his face a fast-forwarded version of what Heath would see in the mirror in twenty more years.

"How are you going into the game?" he asked, rubbing his hands together as if he were getting down to work. "What's your plan?"

Heath cleaned off the rest of the espresso and wondered if there was any statute of limitations on how long you had to explain yourself to a parent.

Although to be fair, the question might not bug him so much if Heath had a better strategy.

"I've gone into every game like it's just a game and it's served me well so far. I played the World Series the same way I played rec ball or a Triple A matchup during spring training." He'd been quoted on it before because his perspective was unique, but it had worked for him. "It keeps the nerves down, and it helps me focus on fundamentals."

Because at the end of the day, that was what baseball was about. Bat on the ball for offense. Glove on the ball for defense.

"Son." His father hunkered down in his chair and

leaned closer. "You can't coach like you played. That mentality worked for you personally on the field as a player. That doesn't mean it's going to work for all your guys. See the big picture and think about what *they* need to hear. Think about each and every one of those guys in the locker room and ask yourself, what does this kid need to know before he goes out there?"

For a second, the message buzzed around Heath's head as if it might make some sense.

"You never coached." He didn't mean it as a slam. But it made him curious why his father would offer the advice. "How do you know what I should be doing?"

His father leaned back from the table.

"I don't." Picking up his Stars' cap, he put it back on his head. "In fact, I think coaching isn't all that different from raising kids, and I effed that up, too. But there are lessons to be learned from mistakes, Heath. And I can tell you right now that sometimes you need to open your damn eyes and see what's in front of you. Before you lose it, you ought to ask yourself, what does that person need? Or, in your case, what does each member of the team need?"

Standing, Mark took his latte and slapped Heath on the back before Heath could begin to untangle what his father had just said.

"You're leaving?" Obviously he'd ticked off his dad, but he had too much on his mind today to figure out what he'd done wrong now.

"I'll let you get back to what you were doing." His

cagey look said he knew that had been exactly nothing. "I'll see you at the game, son. Good luck out there."

Shit.

Another strikeout with the people around him. And Heath wasn't any closer to answers now than he had been before. He still felt edgy and uneasy.

Off.

He could go back up to the hotel room and look through Amber's notes to get some ideas for what he'd say to the guys before what could easily be the last game of his life. But something told Heath the discontent brewing inside him didn't have jack to do with his plans for the team or lack thereof, no matter what his father said.

He had his head on sideways today, and the reason had to do with the woman lying in his bed. A woman he wanted, even though he'd told himself she would be better off without the upheaval, the travel and the scrutiny that came with his life. He had good reasons for sending her safely back to Boston. For once, he wasn't being selfish and was thinking about what was best for someone else.

He just hadn't gotten used to how it felt to make the altruistic decision. Judging by the ache in his chest and the cluttered thoughts in his brain, he damn well didn't like it.

It was a hell of a way to go into the most important game of his career, and he couldn't help feeling a little superstitious, as if he'd somehow jinxed the outcome already.

"So you're dating the manager."

The catcher's wife, Naomi Benoit Davis, asked a simple enough question as she helped herself to the continental breakfast in a private room reserved for the Aces and their families.

Amber followed along behind the petite redhead, filling a plate with fresh fruit and carbs. The private suite was large, so even though there were ten other people having breakfast—coaches and travel staff, mostly—they weren't close enough to anyone else to be overheard.

Naomi had approached her in the hall outside the breakfast room, having apparently been briefed by her husband about Amber's relationship with Heath. Amber remembered they'd ridden up in the elevator with Brody Davis when they first arrived at the hotel. He'd been the one who joked about usually having his wife glued to his side when they traveled.

"It's complicated," Amber answered finally, unwilling to compromise Heath's privacy by kissing and telling.

The redhead stopped in the middle of slathering jelly on her toast. A heart-shaped amethyst barrette winked in the overhead lights as she turned.

"Isn't it always?" Naomi nodded toward a vacant table near a window overlooking the shopping district nearby. "Want to have a seat?"

For a moment, Amber considered making excuses. She wanted to e-mail Rochelle, and she was curious if her editor had sent her any news about her department even though she was on vacation. But hadn't she committed to not overthinking? That ought to apply to hanging out with a potential new friend and not just her relationships with men. This week, she'd proven she could take risks.

Besides, she wasn't so sure she'd be returning to the book reviewing job when this vacation was over. Watching Heath's frustrations with his career made her think about her own. Was it worth sacrificing all her free time for the sake of job security? Maybe she could find another productive outlet for her skills that wouldn't make her feel so anxious all the time and rob her of a social life.

"That would be nice." Amber followed the other woman to the table and set down her dish and a cup of tea. "I'm keeping an eye out for Diego Estes's girlfriend, though. She should be easy to spot since she'll be with a baby."

Diego had called the hotel room this morning after Heath had left her to wake up alone. While she'd had half a mind to hop a plane back home since he had already checked out on her emotionally, Amber hadn't wanted to abandon the team, crazy as that sounded.

She wanted to see Diego hit one out of the park for his son. And she had to admit she was a little curious how Heath would handle the team today. Would he think about any of the research she'd done?

When the young third baseman had asked her to help his girlfriend, Jasmine, find her way to the ballpark, of course she'd said yes. As it turned out, she'd been more invested in Heath's player than Heath had been in her. And that hurt.

"I'm so glad you're doing this." Naomi reached across the table and squeezed Amber's wrist. "I've been telling Brody all season that the team would be a happier place for the guys if there was some more feminine influence. A manager's wife to coordinate some events for the players' wives every now and then."

Amber's spoon clattered into her dish, the word *wife* catching her off guard.

"We're not—that is, Heath and I just barely started dating." And from what she could tell, they were also just barely broken up.

The ache in her chest returned with a vengeance.

"Of course! Sorry to stick my foot in it so fast," Naomi hurried to reassure her. "Don't mind me. I don't mean to have you married already. I just think it's great that you're looking after Diego's girlfriend."

Naomi broke off in the middle of her sentence; her silver Celtic bracelets jingling as she suddenly lifted her hand to point. "This must be her."

Amber turned to see a young, dark-haired woman enter the room, cradling a sleeping infant in one arm. The woman wore jeans and a black blazer with a series of skinny gold chains to fill in the neckline. The baby's blanket was blue and gray, covered with the Aces' logo.

"Jasmine?" Amber rose at the same time as Naomi, the two of them descending on Diego's girlfriend to *ooh* and *ahh* over the tiny baby born just six weeks earlier.

Introductions were made over the child's sleeping head as Amber quizzed her about her flight and whether she'd had any rest.

"Come and sit with us," she urged, pointing out their table. "I can hold Alex if you'd like to grab a plate."

In no time, the infant was handed off to her and the new mom went with Naomi to secure some breakfast. As Amber stood there, holding the smallest baby anyone had ever entrusted her with, she felt her heart knot up in her chest. What would it be like to be part of a family like this, where women handed you their babies and trusted you to care for them? Where players looked to her for help with their personal lives so they could do what they did best out on the field?

Her book knowledge had served a bunch of strange purposes this week. Right now, she had the oddest sensation that she'd been studying up for a position she could have been perfect for if only things had been different between her and Heath.

"Amber?"

Behind her, a few more players had entered the breakfast room with Heath among them. He paused near the entrance, his eyes inscrutable as he studied her.

"Is that Diego's kid?" He peered down into the blanket at Alex's tawny skin and dark hair that formed a V in the middle of his forehead, a handsome carbon copy of his father.

"Yes. Diego talked Jasmine into flying up last night and I told him I'd help look after her today until she gets settled with the other players' wives and girlfriends."

She gestured toward Brody's wife as she steered Jasmine to the coffee bar. "I considered leaving this morning after what you said about going our separate ways once the team lost. But I realized I really wanted to be here to cheer on the team."

Frowning, Heath tugged on her sleeve, urging her deeper into the recesses of the room.

"You thought about taking off today? Before the game?" His brows knitted together, his forehead wrinkling in concern. "I told you I'd take care of everything. For that matter, if we win tonight, we can go out and celebrate anywhere you choose."

"No." She put her answer out there before she let herself think about how nice it would be to languish in Heath's arms, savoring all the feelings he inspired inside her. Logic told her that the longer she spent with him, the more painful it would be to walk away.

That wasn't overthinking. That was a truth it had come time to face.

"Why not?" At least he sounded as frustrated as she felt.

"Because relationships aren't just about being together when things are good—only if you win. That's not how it works."

Behind her, a few more players who called greetings to Heath as they entered and he nodded at them in return. Then, lowering his voice, he focused on her again.

"You promised me three days. Maybe it's a mistake to quit this—" he struggled for the right words

"—*relationship* until we at least give it that much time."

Alex made a sleepy sigh and flexed a tiny fist, his warm body snuggled against her giving her courage to fight for the kind of happiness she deserved. Hadn't she entreated Diego to fight for Jasmine? She'd read enough of *The Mating Season* to know when a relationship was real and worth the effort.

"My feelings for you have changed." She found it difficult to admit, knowing her emotions were not returned. "I got into this thinking I could gain back some self-confidence and start taking a few chances in life. And I've had so much fun—"

"So have I." He reached for her, taking his shoulders in his hands and pouring all of that Heath-intensity into her as he met her gaze. "This week should have sucked, given the way my career is falling apart, but our time together in Nantucket and even here has been... incredible."

Her heart melted and she felt herself swaying. Thankfully, Naomi was marching into her range of vision, waving a cell phone to snag her attention.

"Excuse me." Brody's wife grinned at Heath and then turned to Amber. "I just wanted to see if you'd like to ride over to the game with all the players' wives?"

Another reminder of what she would have to leave behind tonight.

"That would be great. Thank you."

"And you're okay with the baby?" Naomi peeked

into the blanket once more, an expression of maternal longing evident.

"I'm fine, unless you want to take him—"

Naomi had him scooped up and nestled under one arm before she finished the sentence.

"I'll take good care of the little guy," she assured Amber before she backed up a step. "Sorry to interrupt!"

Amber waited until she was certain they wouldn't be overheard.

"I know you're already making plans for what happens when you leave the team. But they need you right now and you're still in charge." She knew it wasn't her business, but damn it, she was making it her business. "And when I said that these past few days have been fun, I was only just beginning. It's been more than fun for me."

Her voice cracked and she knew that any attempt at maintaining her aloof and studious bookworm facade was long gone. The sensitive soul inside had broken through.

She had no idea if Heath could see that, however. He'd admired her for being forthright with him in the past, but maybe he only liked the side of her that could give as good as she got—a side that was more of a protective coating over the tenderhearted romantic she hid inside.

"I don't understand." Heath shook his head. "Isn't that a good thing? Doesn't that prove my point that we should spend more time together?"

"I don't want to spend more time running away from the team or the past or real life." What had started out as a way to thumb her nose at Brent had snowballed into something so much more profound. "I'm falling for you, Heath. And I can't pretend that it's just been a few days of fun."

He rocked back on his heels, so visibly surprised she would have had to laugh if she hadn't been utterly mortified.

"Yo, Skip!" One of Heath's players jogged over to them, his heavy necklace swinging around his neck. "The bench coach is looking for you, and one of the trainers said to let you know we can take some swings before the home team starts batting practice if we get to the field early enough."

"I'll be right there," Heath said without even looking up.

The player rubbed tired eyes. "Sure thing, Skip."

"I know you have to get ready." Amber was glad for the interruption, not sure she could have handled Heath's stunned silence any longer. "I just wanted you to know why it's best for me to make my own way home after the game."

"Amber, wait." He gripped her wrist to hold her in place.

"I'm sorry." She cut him off, knowing she'd put him in an awkward position. "You've got too much on your mind to deal with this now. Good luck today."

She flexed up on her toes to kiss him on the cheek,

an awkward goodbye that wasn't helped by the many pairs of eyes studiously not looking their way.

It was the presence of all those eyes that saved her before she could cave to some compromise of a relationship that would leave her lonely and heartbroken in the end.

Determined to salvage what she could of this day, she hurried toward the gathering throng of players' wives and girlfriends and prepared to cheer on the team for the last time.

15

I'M FALLING FOR YOU.

Amber's words were all Heath could think about as game time neared. He'd had ten guys in his face after the end of his conversation with her at the team breakfast, all wanting a piece of him. Refusing to shove his foot any further in his mouth than he had after revealing his plan to cut and run if he got axed, Heath had let Amber go.

Now, sitting in a courtesy office outside the visiting team locker room an hour before the first pitch, he tried to figure out how to get through this game. His third baseman hadn't slept all night, his twelve-million-dollar-a-year reliever had been in the strip clubs until dawn, and the team as a whole was wired from tension Heath himself had undoubtedly passed along to them.

It wouldn't be news to anyone on the team that they were all underperforming—Heath included. But he didn't have a clue what to say to fire them up.

I'm falling for you.

Heath pounded the empty desk with his fist, knowing he was missing something here, but damned if he could figure out what. Amber told him she was falling for him and in the same breath she'd accused him of running out on the team. If that was the case, how could she fall for someone like that?

Out in the locker room, he could hear the guys talking and laughing. He had no doubt Chase Montoya was holding court in one corner, telling the rookies how many bottles of Veuve Clicquot and Cristal he'd wasted on exotic dancers who would have no doubt appreciated cash more than the alcohol.

Other than that predictable patter, the locker room was actually kind of quiet. Heath knew he'd been tagged as more of a "players' coach" since coming on board in Boston, letting the veteran guys take a leading role to help shape the team. Once a veteran himself, Heath had appreciated managers who weren't hard-asses about mindless hours of infield practice or forcing big hitters to bunt around a run in some pea-brained excuse for strategy.

But hearing Montoya's guffaws in the other room made him wonder if he'd been too lenient. Too much of a player when he should have been more of a leader.

His hand went to his shirt pocket, where he'd tucked a few sheets of paper containing Amber's notes from the library last night. Her handwriting flowed neatly over the page, compact and graceful, each line dovetailing smoothly into the next.

From the middle of the page, a quote jumped out

at him. A tidbit from famed Dodger coach, Tommy Lasorda. "About the only problem with success is that it does not teach you how to deal with failure."

Funny how sometimes an obvious truth could whack you upside the head with implications you'd never seen. Because that quote was all about him—Heath Donovan—in a nutshell.

Heath had been a success all his life. Some sports writers had termed it "phenomenal success," and if that didn't go to your head, what would? But maybe all the success in the world had been piss-poor preparation for this moment. He needed to reinvent the wheel, and he needed to do it today.

Standing, he clutched Amber's notes tighter in his hand, hoping there was something in there that would speak to his team as loudly as those words spoke to him. He didn't have a plan, per se. But he had his eyes open in a way they hadn't been all season.

His father's harping on him had helped. But Amber's generosity—both with her heart and with her time—had driven the message home.

He wasn't going to fail her or the team today. Because starting right now, he wouldn't just be another successful player at the helm. He was officially taking charge.

He was the leader. The manager. And right now, the Aces were still his team.

AMERICA'S PASTIME WOULD have seemed like a great way to spend a summer afternoon if Amber's heart hadn't been fractured at the seams. It didn't help that the Aces had played eight innings of baseball in the past three hours and were down by a run as they headed up to bat in the ninth.

The sun had slipped down in the sky but remained visible over the open-air stadium, throwing just the right amount of warmth on her bare arms and legs as she sat in her cargo shorts and navy blue Aces tank top. The shirt had been an unexpected gift from Naomi Davis, the catcher's wife. She'd decided Amber's arrival in their group deserved to be celebrated and she'd bought out the gift shop's small supply of visiting team apparel to give a matching shirt to all the players' significant others.

The glittery heart around the Aces' logo was decidedly girly and nothing Amber would have chosen, which made her love it all the more. She felt like a different person than the one she'd been just one short week ago, and her ultrafeminine tank top broadcast a new confidence to the world. She wasn't going to hole up in her apartment any longer, working hours on end for the sake of her job. The new Amber was all about balance.

Too bad the new and improved Amber didn't date guys who were only looking for a fling. Why couldn't Heath see they could handle something more?

"Get your peanuts! Get your popcorn!" A teenager carrying a tray full of snacks tromped through the stands, his red and white striped paper hat tilted over one eye.

Next to Amber, Diego's girlfriend twitched in her seat as the first Aces batter grounded out and the next popped up.

Two outs.

"We could still win this game." Jasmine had been optimistic from the start, even when Diego had struck out twice before getting a walk in the sixth. "You wait. My man won't leave this park without lighting up this pitcher."

Amber smiled, thinking Jasmine was as crazy about Diego as he obviously was about her. She could picture them together for the long haul—her toting around a cute clan of kids to his games, him doing anything in his power to make her happy. Amber had already overheard Jasmine asking around about the team's charity involvement and good works' projects. Apparently, the woman had a lot to give in that department. No doubt, the Aces would have some serious resources for her to sink her teeth into.

Why couldn't a future for Amber and Heath be just as possible?

She couldn't imagine going back to her walls of white books for company after being exposed to the riot of colors and people in Heath's world.

She could have a place here. It wasn't a big, splashy spot like Jasmine would undoubtedly make for herself. But Amber could easily envision a role where she coordinated some trips out with the women who normally only saw each other at games. This group would benefit from a few activities together to prevent them from feeling isolated.

Amber knew firsthand how isolation led to insecurity. If her mother had had more of a network around her, maybe she wouldn't have been so quick to fall apart when Amber's father had left. For that matter, if Amber hadn't allowed herself to become so isolated in her world of books—much as she enjoyed them—maybe she wouldn't have been so devastated by Brent's defection.

Damn it, this was what Rochelle had been telling her ever since college. If it had taken her ten years to see, maybe Amber shouldn't expect Heath to recognize something that was obvious to her in just a few days.

Regret nipped at her for piling more grief on his worries with the team. Could she have chosen worse timing? But she hadn't wanted to repeat the mistakes she'd made in the past, coasting along without committing her heart half so much as her head. Heath had touched her deeply and she'd wanted him to know it.

"Amber Nichols?" A fresh-faced bat boy with a baseball cap pulled way down to his eyebrows stood at the end of the seating reserved for the players' families.

"I'm Amber Nichols." She raised her hand to draw the boy's eye.

"This is for you." He passed her a piece of paper and then darted back toward the field where he slid through the bars next to the dugout.

An usher standing guard nearby didn't even raise an eyebrow.

Snap!

The crack of a bat made her look up. As one, all the players' wives and girlfriends leaned forward in their seats to watch the progress of a ball through the infield.

"Single." Naomi Davis let out a whoop followed by something that sounded like a war cry. "We'll take it, baby!"

Apparently her husband had been at bat as the catcher now stood on first base.

Still, one runner on base wasn't going to make up for a one-run deficit in the ninth when they already had two outs. Amber's time in L.A.—her time with Heath—was running out.

"Well?" Jasmine elbowed Amber. "Are you going to open it?"

She nodded pointedly at the paper in her hands, the paper Amber had half forgotten.

"Yes." Her heart pounded harder, knowing that only Heath would have sent her a note.

"The managers never like cell phones or texting in the dugout," one of the other women in a seat behind her clarified.

Unfolding the paper that was actually a preprinted form for a player roster, Amber read the handwritten scrawl on the blank side.

I haven't been seeing the big picture—on the field or off. But that's changing starting right now. Win or lose, I want to be with you. Please meet me in the players' parking garage after the game. I'll be out as fast as I can.

Her hand shook. She knew because the paper trembled in her fingers. Did he really mean that about wanting to be with her? Or was he just hoping to slow her exit after the game so they could talk?

Either way, a small spark of hope flamed to life inside her, and the day took on new possibility.

"Yes!" the wives screamed all around her.

For a moment, the enthusiastic cries felt like a chorus cheering the good news.

Then, Naomi put an inside-out baseball hat on Amber's head.

"It's a two-out rally, girl. Get your rally cap on."

Her emotions were all knotted up, but she'd said she was here to cheer Heath's team on and she planned to do just that.

Did he really want to be with her, win or lose?

She wondered as Diego Estes came up to bat.

"He hasn't had a hit in three games," Jasmine reminded everyone around her before she kissed Alex's head. She stood up, baby in her arms, as if Diego would see her. "It's your turn, Diego! Go get yours!"

The batter never looked her way, but he took one hand off the bat before he settled into his stance, and pointed right at her in the stands as if he knew exactly where the mother of his child stood.

Amber's heart warmed to see that connection, a bond that twenty-four hours ago Diego had been scared he'd never feel again. If these two could overcome distance and hurt on both sides to support each other, Amber wanted to believe she and Heath could fight their way through whatever life threw at them.

Win or lose...

Diego fouled off one ball and then another. Two strikes.

They were one strike away from going home when Diego delivered on Jasmine's faith in him. He smacked a fastball so hard and so straight into centerfield, Amber feared for whoever was seated in those upper decks.

Screams erupted all around her. Even Alex woke up to make some noise while his mother hooted and hollered.

Amber was thrilled for the team and for Heath. But it wasn't over yet. The best of the Stars' batting order would still come up to the plate in the bottom of the ninth.

Unfortunately, the pitcher due up on the mound was the Aces' veteran closer, Chase Montoya, the same player who'd closed down the strip clubs the night before, according to rumor. If Heath was seeing the big picture right now, he had to know they were in one heck of a tight spot.

CLEARLY, HEATH'S commitment to a new coaching style was being tested.

He'd told Amber that "win or lose" he wanted to be with her, and he meant it with every fiber of his being. But he preferred to win, and fate had handed him a two-run inning after two outs. Normally, an Aces' lead meant one thing..."Money" Montoya. His star reliever had successfully closed out the first fifteen games of the year before losing momentum in midseason. The highly paid veteran had flat-out squandered leads in three consecutive games.

Still, conventional baseball wisdom said you went with your big-money closer.

But middle reliever Dave Bryant had just thrown a perfect one-two-three eighth, striking out two of three batters and retiring the other on a feeble tapper back to the mound. Bryant was in a groove. Furthermore, Montoya had opted to party all night and spread the culture of fast living to a bunch of neophyte players who looked up to him.

Stop being the players' coach. Be a leader, damn it.

He could almost picture that neat writing of Amber's on the folded paper in his pocket. "If you're in control, they're in control." He was pretty sure that one came from Tom Landry. Heath hoped like hell it was true when the dugout phone rang with the bullpen coach asking if he wanted Montoya.

"I'm sticking with Bryant."

Next to the phone on the bullpen monitor permanently fixed on the opposite side of the outfield wall, Donovan could see Montoya kick the dirt on his way back to the bench, that big rope of a chain swinging around his neck. No turning back now. Montoya was no longer in the mindset of closing out games, and would likely demand a trade as soon as this one ended. He was never a team-first player.

Still, two bad pitches and Heath could start thinking about a career after managing baseball. He half wished Amber knew what a monumental decision this was for him. For the team. Then again, if Naomi Davis still had her ear, she'd probably fill her in fast enough. The catcher's wife knew as much about the sport as him.

Fully committed now, Heath turned his attention to the mound. Bryant had dominated the competition as the saves leader at Triple A the previous season. Still, the lineup on deck—Robins, Sorilla and Kazan—was as formidable as any in the game.

"You gotta know the shit's gonna hit the fan after this, Skip," the bench coach observed between chews on his tobacco. Grizzled and gray, the Aces' second-in-command had been a coach when the elder Donovan had played, so that told Heath he had to be nearing retirement.

"It already has." Heath wasn't going to defend himself. There was a new era in this dugout if he stuck around the team past tonight, and it was just as well everyone knew it.

"Shane Robins is a slap hitter," the old bench coach, Butch Casey, observed. "More infield hits than anyone in baseball this season. A well-placed bunt along the third baseline and forget it, the leadoff hitter is on."

Heath sorely wished the old guy would focus on his chew. Ideally, a bench coach was more for bouncing around strategy ideas, not articulating a manager's worst fears. But there you had it. Heath's job hadn't come with the ability to pick his own coaches.

"Always a possibility," Heath agreed amiably, hungering for a view over the dugout to see Amber in the stands.

Turning back to the game, Bryant appeared determined to pitch the speedster inside. Donovan knew that although Montoya had better pitches than Bryant, Bryant's command was superior, as he could pinpoint his location in the strike zone. And that was exactly what he did, retiring Robins on a harmless grounder to the first baseman.

The dugout gave a cursory round of shouts and encouragement, the mood among the guys surprised. Confused. No doubt every one in there was second-guessing this new management style.

"I don't think you'll get off that easy with Jose Sorilla," Butch observed, standing at the fence and breathing his tobacco-scented words of doom in Heath's ear. "He's had thirty home runs and thirty stolen bases in the same season, a rare breed. And for a right-handed hitter, he's especially hard on lefties."

"Heard and understood, Butch." Heath knew if he was going to get second-guessed for his decision to not use the closer, Sorilla was the reason why.

However, catcher Brody Davis had a thorough understanding of Bryant's pitching capabilities as well as the batter's style. Once again, Bryant spotted the pitch exactly where the catcher set up—at the knees and on the outside corner.

Sorilla swung violently at the pitch, pulling a shot down the line that landed cleanly in Diego Estes's waiting glove. The home crowd cheers quickly turned into groans.

Then, silence.

Heath actually started to hope.

"It's not too late to send in Montoya," Butch told him in low, confidential tones. "Bryant still has to face Kevin Kazan."

Not even know-it-all Butch felt the need to give Kevin "Bam Bam" Kazan's stats. The guy was primarily an all-or-nothing batter, having homered or struck out in sixty-five percent of his at-bats. Kazan, who led the league in home runs, was not the guy to make a bad pitch to.

"I'm not yanking Bryant." He wasn't giving up on someone who was working hard and doing everything Heath could have asked of him.

It was a hell of a lot more than he could say for Montoya. And, as messages to the team went, this one decision was going to speak louder than any locker room speech or postgame pep talk he could have crafted.

Amber's quotes and research hadn't been meant for spouting to his players anyway, though he hadn't realized it at the time. They'd been the final ammunition to help him understand what his father had been telling him. See the whole field.

God, he couldn't wait to tell her how much she'd helped him today.

On the mound, Bryant went to work, firing one ball after another. The kid walked Kazan on four straight pitches, and putting the tying run on base in the process.

Heath could already hear the criticisms weakly veiled as questions in the postgame press conference... *Why stick with Bryant after he walked Kazan on four pitches? Why not bring in Montoya at that point? Wasn't it evident that Bryant was choking/tiring/ill-suited for the closer role?*

Nonetheless, Heath was determined to stick with his newly appointed closer, a decision that grew even more questionable when he fired a wild pitch to the Stars' next hitter in the lineup and "Bam Bam" advanced to second. Now, a single could tie the game and effectively put the winning run on base.

"This one's a pesky hitter," Butch announced, pointing to Micah Bailey at the plate.

But before the old guy could start in on stats that Heath already knew, star pitcher Jay Cannon moved closer to Heath at the rail and whooped it up for the young gun on the mound.

Well, damn. Except for Amber's sighs in his ear, Heath couldn't dream up a sweeter sound at this moment in time.

Jay Cannon was probably the only guy on the team pulling down more dough than Montoya. His support told everyone in the dugout—loud and clear—that he supported Heath.

There were victories on this day, damn it, no matter what the final outcome.

Still, after two consecutive balls, it looked as if

Bryant needed a pep talk. Just the kind of thing Heath sucked at.

He rubbed the paper in his pocket, thinking Amber would have something smart to say, even if she copped it out of a book. The woman knew to go to the experts, unlike stubborn former ballplayers who thought they knew everything. Heath walked as slowly as possible out to the pitching rubber, not quite sure what words to use.

Brody Davis jogged up to the mound, too, pulling up his catcher's mask, his face intent.

Heath took a second to glance up into the stands, knowing his dad was up there somewhere. Amber, too, although he knew she'd be sitting directly behind him right now.

"Davis, you got any ideas on pitches?" Heath figured he'd ask the experts. Just like Amber had showed him.

The catcher shrugged. "I thought maybe the changeup?"

"Sounds good."

Bryant didn't look one bit reassured by the talk. He wiped the sweat off his forehead with a corner of his shirt. "What's the scouting report on this guy? How does he do with the changeup?"

Heath shook his head. "This game isn't about what *he* can do, it's about what *you* can do. The ball is in your hands, tiger, and you wouldn't be my closer today if you couldn't get out of situations like this. Don't worry about him. Just let it fly and hit Brody's mitt."

He clapped the kid on the shoulder and let the pitcher

and catcher get back to work. Walking away from the mound, Heath peered up into the stands above the dugout and spotted Amber with ease, as if his gaze was for her alone.

Thank God she was still sitting there, right in the middle of about twelve women—mostly wives but a couple of girlfriends—who frequently came to the games. She belonged here. With him.

He'd import books from all over the globe to keep her by his side. Hell, he'd hire a staffer to cover them all in white dust jackets, too.

She didn't give him a reassuring smile, but she didn't flip him off, either. And the fact that she was still here gave him more hope than his sorry ass deserved.

As he ducked back into the dugout, the game resumed.

The next pitch was a knee-high fastball that Bailey could only pound into the ground—right back at Bryant. He fielded the one-hopper and threw to first for the out.

Game over.

Heath's team had just won the single most important game of his career as a manager. He was so damn proud of his guys he choked up like a girl when Jay Cannon pounded him on the back. The dugout went wild, sensing a shift in momentum that was going to do them a whole lot of good.

But if Amber Nichols wouldn't give him another chance, this win wasn't going to mean jack in that big picture that Heath now saw all too clearly.

16

AMBER WATCHED A LIMOUSINE pull up to the curb in the players' parking lot just at the same moment Heath plowed through the doors into the underground garage.

He wore shorts and an Aces' T-shirt, his hair slick against his head as if he'd just stepped out of the shower. He looked just like he had that first day she'd seen him on the beach in Nantucket.

If ever there was an ideal man for a fling...

She remembered thinking that the first time she saw him. Her heart lodged in her throat now, however, since she wanted much more than a fling.

He spotted her and gave a nod toward the chauffeur hopping out of the limo, even though he never took his eyes off her.

"I dialed up a ride for you." Heath jogged to shorten the distance between them. The stark expression on his face would have never given away the fact that his team had won a significant game less than an hour earlier.

His job was safe. He'd proven his worth and more to the Aces' owners.

"A ride for me?" She hoped she hadn't misunderstood his note during the game. "You're not going with me?"

The players' garage was quiet on this side of the elevator bank since most of the players drove their own vehicles and used the valet service. A few taxis waited, but no fans thanks to excellent security.

It was so quiet, Amber's question echoed back to her off the concrete walls.

"More than anything, I want to go wherever you're going." He waved off the chauffeur who had just opened the door for them, probably so they could talk in private. "But I want you to have the option of kicking me to the curb for being too stubborn and blind to see that you weren't a groupie and that this wasn't just a temporary thing."

Her heart swelled that he would do something so incredibly thoughtful. It was also sweetly insightful to let her feel as if she had the decision-making power after Brent had made her feel so insignificant.

She drifted a step closer to Heath.

"It's been quite a few days since you thought I was a groupie." Their time together had been fast and intense. The most exciting days of her life. "I don't think I can keep holding that against you."

His eyes were so steady on her that her heart tripped up in its rhythm.

"Still, I want you to have the choice of taking this

free ride wherever you choose, even if you want to head to the airport and back home. I've been so busy living in the moment—riding the wave of success I had as a player—that I didn't see I'm thirty-eight years old and it's past time to take a long view on my career, my life and the people in it."

Amber saw a few guys emerge from the elevators and she waved Heath into the backseat of the limo.

"Why don't we at least sit inside where it's private?" She hopped up into the back and then slid into one of the leather seats.

Her living room didn't have much more square footage than the vehicle's spacious interior. As Heath settled in next to her, however, the space shrank. She might as well have been tucked inside a broom closet with him since her whole body tingled with awareness.

His scent was familiar to her by now. His thigh rested mere inches from hers and she could imagine the heat they would generate if they closed that distance.

"Congratulations on keeping the team," she blurted, feeling guilty she hadn't mentioned it yet. "I've been so preoccupied since I got your note or I would have said something sooner. Plus, I don't know enough about baseball to really appreciate what you did, but Naomi said—"

Heath laughed. "I had the feeling she'd see the nuances at work. Chase Montoya wasn't too happy with me that I didn't put him in, but I thought it was a good time to send a message to the guys about what I expect from them. I'm not going to manage like a player anymore."

"You rewarded hard work." She could understand that much. "But it seemed like a risky time to test out a new approach."

"If not then, when?" He pulled out a folded sheet of paper from the thigh pocket of his shorts. "I was looking at these quotes you gave me before the game and there was one about success not preparing you for failure."

"I remember it." She studied him more carefully, beginning to see there was more at work here than just him lobbying for more time together.

"It made me think about how much I've learned to trust my instincts." He set the paper on a low side table. "That worked well as a player. Not so much as a manager. Or in relationships."

He'd thought about her today, during the most crucial game of his managing career. That alone would have touched her. But the fact that he seemed to want to make her happy gave her heart palpitations.

His thigh loomed so close. His big hand rested on his knee, and she thought about how it would feel to place her palm inside his.

"So you changed how you managed." She was starting to see the significance of what he'd done today by keeping in the relief pitcher.

Yes, it had been about baseball. But it represented a deeper shift in thinking. An openness to new ideas.

"Yes." He moved the hand closest to her, stretching that arm out along the back of her seat, without really touching her. "Not that I see myself as ever turning into a really hard-core, old-school tough guy or anything. But I'm not going to just blindly follow my instincts. I'm going to question everything, study traditional strategy and see where I can improve. More important, I'm not going to just assume that I can't make things work with you on a long-term basis because of my job."

Behind her, Heath's hand came to rest on her braid where it snaked along the seat. She could feel the gentle tug against her scalp as he slid his fingers very lightly up and down the woven center.

Her heart stuck in her throat, and her skin hummed with pleasurable shivers.

"Long-term?" Her breathless voice didn't sound like it belonged to her.

"I screwed up a marriage." He slid under the braid to cup her shoulder in one hand. "That doesn't mean I will always mess up relationships. I know how to dig in and work harder."

He used the tail of her braid like a paintbrush to trace patterns along her bare arm. Had he leaned closer? Amber couldn't quite breathe. Either that, or she was holding her breath waiting for him to kiss her.

"I would like that," she managed, hypnotized by the promise in his dark eyes. "In fact, I really want to be around to see you dig in and work hard."

His hand stilled in the middle of the mesmerizing patterns he'd been making along her arm.

"Are you sure?"

"Completely sure."

"Because this is one instance where overthinking could be a good thing."

Closing the gap between them, she edged over that last inch on the seat until her thigh brushed his and her hip bumped him.

"I've already thought about it enough." She stroked his cheek with shaky fingers, hardly daring to believe she might have shared her heart with a man who wanted to take really good care of it. "While I'm glad you're trying to be more analytical sometimes, you have to know that other times, I'd very much like you to trust your instincts."

A feral grin quirked his lips as he banged on the roof of the limo. Instantly, the driver set the vehicle in motion.

"In that case, we're going to a little beach house I know." He was already pulling the band out of her braid to free her hair.

"Not Nantucket?" They still had two games to play on the west coast.

"No, a little place on Catalina Island." Gently, he slid one strap of her tank top off her shoulder. "It's far away from everyone and everything."

Amber relaxed into his touch, her skin coming alive everywhere he stroked.

"You don't think the team will mind?"

"I don't care who thinks what." He kissed her bare collarbone as the limo picked up speed. "I called the Aces' owner and told him I'm not dancing to his tune anymore. He's not going to be breathing down my neck until at least next year. And as for the rest of the guys, a little worry about the new regime will do them good tonight."

Amber would have Heath all to herself, just like that first night in Nantucket when he helped her see the depth of passion that lurked inside her.

"I like the new regime," she observed, tugging at the neckline of her shirt in an effort to be free of any clothes in the way of Heath's hot, persuasive mouth. "In fact, I've come to a few of the same realizations about my own work, too."

"Really?"

"Management's been breathing down my neck quite a bit, too." She hadn't thought about it in quite those terms, but the metaphor was apt. "I've been running so hard to keep my job for the past six months that I haven't really thought about if it's making me happy anymore. And as much as I love the work, it's too much."

He frowned, shifting back from her as if to gauge her expression. "You're thinking about leaving the book reviewing business?"

"I can look for another outlet for my reviews. Or find something else for my unique skill set. There must be jobs available somewhere for a book geek."

"Maybe," he began, shifting closer again, "you could look for a job that you could do from anywhere. In case, you know, you felt like doing some traveling in the near future." He kissed a line from her cheek to her ear and down her neck, inciting shivers.

"I'll admit, I like flying first-class." She tipped her

head, enjoying the way sensations chased down her spine.

"Then I'm going to show you the time of your life during the course of eighty-one road games."

"That's a lot of travel." Days full of endless possibilities by Heath's side.

"There's going to be a lot of time in hotels, just you and me." He laid her all the way down on the seat, his body half covering hers. "I hope you don't get bored seeing me all the time."

"And I hope you don't get tired of me telling you how to run your team when I don't know anything about baseball." She stared up at him, her lover turned lifetime love, and felt more complete than she'd ever been in her whole life.

He grinned as his hips settled against hers.

"I don't know how we'll do with the team, but I'm going to have a winning streak where you're concerned," he promised. "You wait and see."

* * * * *

COMING NEXT MONTH

Available August 31, 2010

REQUEST YOUR FREE BOOKS!

2 FREE NOVELS
PLUS 2
FREE GIFTS!

HARLEQUIN®

Blaze™

Red-hot reads!

HB10R

HARLEQUIN®

A Romance

FOR EVERY MOOD™

Spotlight on
— Heart & Home —

Heartwarming romances
where love can happen
right when you least expect it.

See the next page to enjoy a sneak peek
from Harlequin Superromance®,
a Heart and Home series.

CATHHHSR10

Enjoy a sneak peek at fan favorite Molly O'Keefe's
Harlequin Superromance miniseries,
THE NOTORIOUS O'NEILLS, *with*
TYLER O'NEILL'S REDEMPTION,
available September 2010
only from Harlequin Superromance.

Police chief Juliette Tremblant recognized the shape of the man strolling down the street—in as calm and leisurely fashion as if it were the middle of the day rather than midnight. She slowed her car, convinced her eyes were playing tricks on her. It had been a long time since Tyler O'Neill had been seen in this town.

As she pulled to a stop at the curb, he turned toward her, and her heart about stopped.

"What the hell are you doing here, Tyler?"

"Well, if it isn't Juliette Tremblant." He made his way over to her, then leaned down so he could look her in the eye. He was close enough to touch.

Juliette was not, repeat, *not* going to touch Tyler O'Neill. Not with her fingers. Not with a ten-foot pole. There would be no touching. Which was too bad, since it was the only way she was ever going to convince herself the man standing in front of her—as rumpled and heart-stoppingly handsome now as he'd been at sixteen—was real.

And not a figment of all her furious revenge dreams.

"What are you doing back in Bonne Terre?" she asked.

"The manor is sitting empty," Tyler said and shrugged, as though his arriving out of the blue after ten years was casual. "Seems like someone should be watching over the family home."

"You?" She laughed at the very notion of him being here for any unselfish reason. "Please."

HSREXP0910

He stared at her for a second, then smiled. Her heart fluttered against her chest—a small mechanical bird powered by that smile.

"You're right." But that cryptic comment was all he offered.

Juliette bit her lip against the other questions.

Why did you go?

Why didn't you write? Call?

What did I do?

But what would be the point? Ten years of silence were all the answer she really needed.

She had sworn off feeling anything for this man long ago. Yet one look at him and all the old hurt and rage resurfaced as though they'd been waiting for the chance. That made her mad.

She put the car in gear, determined not to waste another minute thinking about Tyler O'Neill. "Have a good night, Tyler," she said, liking all the cool "go screw yourself" she managed to fit into those words.

It seems Juliette has an old score to settle with Tyler.
Pick up TYLER O'NEILL'S REDEMPTION
to see how he makes it up to her.
Available September 2010,
only from Harlequin Superromance.